Delivering the Grocer to His Maker . . .

A sound! Behind him. It was too faint for him to consciously identify and could have been something as innocent as a bird dropping down to the earth, but he was not going to take any chances with such.

He immediately fell into a crouch and spun around, .45 in hand.

A man stood there.

A man with a rifle.

In that instant, Longarm recognized the grocer. The one who had said he had no gun. Yeah, right.

Longarm had a gun, and he was a top hand with it. His Colt spat fire and lead.

The grocer's eyes widened in shock and he staggered backward two tottering paces as a small red stain appeared in the center of his apron bib. The stain spread and flowed as the man's lifeblood drained away until his heart was stopped forever.

He stopped backpedaling, stood upright swaying back and forth for a moment, and then fell facedown into the dirt behind the main street buildings.

He hit hard and made no attempt to soften his fall.

By then Longarm was pressed up against the building where he stood, .45 held at the ready . . .

DON'T MISS THESE ALL-ACTION WESTERN SERIES FROM THE BERKLEY PUBLISHING GROUP

THE GUNSMITH by J. R. Roberts

Clint Adams was a legend among lawmen, outlaws, and ladies. They called him . . . the Gunsmith.

LONGARM by Tabor Evans

The popular long-running series about Deputy U.S. Marshal Custis Long—his life, his loves, his fight for justice.

SLOCUM by Jake Logan

Today's longest-running action Western. John Slocum rides a deadly trail of hot blood and cold steel.

BUSHWHACKERS by B. J. Lanagan

An action-packed series by the creators of Longarm! The rousing adventures of the most brutal gang of cutthroats ever assembled—Quantrill's Raiders.

DIAMONDBACK by Guy Brewer

Dex Yancey is Diamondback, a Southern gentleman turned con man when his brother cheats him out of the family fortune. Ladies love him. Gamblers hate him. But nobody pulls one over on Dex . . .

WILDGUN by Jack Hanson

The blazing adventures of mountain man Will Barlow—from the creators of Longarm!

TEXAS TRACKER by Tom Calhoun

J.T. Law: the most relentless—and dangerous—manhunter in all Texas. Where sheriffs and posses fail, he's the best man to bring in the most vicious outlaws—for a price.

TABOR EVANS

LONGARM AND THE TOWN FULL OF TROUBLE

JOVE BOOKS, NEW YORK

THE BERKLEY PUBLISHING GROUP
Published by the Penguin Group
Penguin Group (USA) Inc.
375 Hudson Street, New York, New York 10014, USA

USA | Canada | UK | Ireland | Australia | New Zealand | India | South Africa | China

Penguin Books Ltd., Registered Offices: 80 Strand, London WC2R 0RL, England
For more information about the Penguin Group, visit penguin.com.

LONGARM AND THE TOWN FULL OF TROUBLE

A Jove Book / published by arrangement with the author

For information, address: The Berkley Publishing Group,
a division of Penguin Group (USA) Inc.,
375 Hudson Street, New York, New York 10014.

ISBN: 978-0-515-15375-0

PUBLISHING HISTORY
Jove mass-market edition / July 2013

PRINTED IN THE UNITED STATES OF AMERICA

10 9 8 7 6 5 4 3 2 1

Cover illustration by Milo Sinovcic.

Chapter 1

"Harder. Harder, darlin' "

"I don't want to hurt you."

"It's all right. I can take it. Do it harder."

"All right," Deputy United States Marshal Custis Long responded. "If you say so."

"Ouch, dammit!"

"I *told* you . . ."

"I know, dear. You did." She smiled. "But at least the shoe came off."

"Damn female," Long muttered. "I don't know why you'd stuff your foot into a shoe that's two sizes too small for you t' begin with."

Deborah smiled. "It's a woman thing, Custis dear. You wouldn't understand."

"You're right about that," he said, standing upright and unbuckling his belt.

Deborah giggled and wriggled her toes for a moment, enjoying the freedom of being barefoot. Then she slipped off the side of the bed and dropped to her knees in front of him.

She reached for the buttons at his fly and expertly undid them, following that by slipping a hand inside Longarm's brown corduroy trousers to find his manhood and pull it out where she could admire it.

"Such a lovely thing," she said. She leaned forward and pressed the hard, bulbous tip of his cock against her cheek. "It has a scent like . . . like seawater, I think. Yes, like seawater."

Longarm arched his back, straining forward to meet her mouth. Deborah ran her tongue up and down his shaft, causing him to shiver with pleasure in response to her touch.

He liked that. Liked even more the sensations when she took him firmly inside her mouth and began to suck.

As a showgirl Deborah was only in the chorus, but as far as he was concerned she had plenty of talent.

"Ah!"

She reached inside his trousers to find his balls and tickle them. Then she scraped a fingernail over his asshole while she continued to suck. With her other hand she reached around behind him. She pulled him closer. Wanting all of him.

Longarm groaned and thrust himself completely into her mouth and beyond, on through into Deborah's throat. He could feel the tight ring of cartilage there engulf him.

Her saliva ran onto his balls, where it cooled.

Deborah made small, snuffling sounds as she grunted and panted and mutely asked for his cum.

Longarm complied, his sperm shooting hot and sticky into her throat.

She let out a small cry and gobbled his juices down.

After several long moments she released him, letting his cock slide wetly out of her mouth. The air that reached his dick felt cold after the heat of Deborah's mouth.

Longarm shuddered. And reached down to put two fingers beneath Deborah's jaw and draw her onto her feet, then backward onto the soft bed that awaited them for the rest of the evening.

He was still hard. She took him in her hand and drew

him down onto her open, eager body. Her pussy dripped with her own juices, easing his entry.

Deborah sighed as Longarm's massive cock filled her.

"Careful now," he whispered, "or I'm gonna be late for work."

"Custis dear, it's ten o'clock at night."

Longarm grinned. "Yeah. I know." And thrust forward, driving himself hard into her.

Chapter 2

Longarm mounted the stone steps to the Federal Building on Denver's Colfax Avenue. The big, gray building was long familiar territory. It practically felt like home to him.

So did the office of Chief U.S. Marshal William Vail—Billy to his friends and employees. Billy's clerk Henry was, as always, bent over his desk, rimless wire glasses perched on his nose, pale eyes searching something among the papers laid out before him.

Henry looked up when Longarm came in. "He wants to see you," Henry said.

"What's up?"

Henry merely shrugged by way of an answer. Longarm knew better than to believe the boss's right hand did not know what Billy wanted, but he did not press the issue.

"Thanks," he said, hanging his hat on an arm of the tall, dark wood coat rack that stood in a corner near Henry's desk.

Longarm stepped over to Billy's door and paused there for a moment to tug the tails of his coat down and run a hand over his hair.

Longarm was a study in browns. Brown hair. Sweeping brown handlebar mustache. Darkly tanned features. Golden brown eyes that could turn as hard and cold as flint if someone crossed him. Brown checked shirt and brown calfskin vest with a gold chain crossing his flat belly from one vest pocket to the other.

He wore brown corduroy trousers and a brown tweed coat, but freshly blacked—he had stopped on the way to work to have a boy tend to them—calf-high cavalry boots and a black gunbelt with a black leather cross-draw holster that held a double-action .45 Colt revolver.

His features were more craggy and sun-blasted than handsome. But more than one young woman seemed to find him interesting.

He was tall, standing somewhere above six feet in height, and had wide shoulders, a narrow waist, and a horseman's powerful legs.

He also had a smile that crinkled the corners of his eyes and caused women to become wet between their legs.

He paused there for only a moment before he reached up and lightly rapped his knuckles on the frosted glass inset in Billy's office door.

"Come," he heard from the other side of the glass.

Longarm entered, carefully closed the door behind him—the glass panel had been replaced not too awfully long ago and he did not know how much force it could take—and presented himself in front of his balding, moon-faced boss.

Billy Vail looked like a pushover, like any ornery yahoo could push the man around. That would be a serious mistake. Vail had once been a Texas Ranger, and a very salty one at that. He could hold his own with the best of them, using fists, knives, or six-guns, never mind his mild looks.

He frowned when he looked up and saw his best deputy ready for duty.

Longarm did not much care for what that extremely serious look implied.

"What is it, Boss? Trouble?"

Chapter 3

"Trouble? Perhaps." Billy spun his chair around so he was facing the window. He sat there for long moments, then turned back around to face Longarm. "What I have here might be termed . . . delicate. I need you to make an arrest and bring the man in for trial. All very straightforward. This fellow stole from the mails. He must be brought in."

"Hell, Billy, that ain't no problem," Longarm began, but Vail cut him off.

"There is more to it," Billy said. "He . . . Like I said, it could be delicate. This man . . . this boy, really . . . is the son of a man who is active in politics. A man who would like to sit in this chair right here."

"He wants to be appointed as U.S. marshal in your place?"

Vail nodded. "Exactly."

"I thought your place was pretty solid," Longarm said. "D'you mind if I smoke?" he asked, reaching inside his coat for a cheroot.

"Not now, Custis."

"Oh. Sorry." Longarm shoved the cheroot back into his inside coat pocket. "Your sinuses acting up again, Boss?"

Vail nodded.

"Sorry," Longarm repeated. "Now about this thief . . ."

After a moment Billy nodded again. "Yes, he is a thief, and that is easy enough to understand. The problem is that if . . . no, I should say when . . . I have him arrested, there will be those who will claim I am acting out of political interests and not simply enforcing the laws."

"Hell, Billy, everybody knows . . ."

"Everybody knows crap," Billy snorted. "When politics comes into the picture, Longarm, common sense flies out. Even when people know the truth, they are apt to distort it for their own personal gain. Some to make those gains themselves, some to toady up to their superiors or to those they think will be advancing politically."

"You think I'm gonna run into some o' that," Longarm said.

"I'm almost certain of it." Billy spun around again to face the window, and toward the window he said, "I don't know, Longarm. I've been in this job a long time now. Maybe it's time for me to retire. Maybe it's time I put my badge away in a drawer and took up living a life of leisure."

"Boss, you're letting this politicking get in the way of *your* common sense. You know, or maybe you don't know, that there's nobody could do this job as good as you. Or as honest an' fair. So quit fretting about that sort o' bullshit an' give me my assignment. I'll find the thieving son of a bitch an' bring him in for trial. That's what we do here, an' we do it mighty damn well if you ask my opinion." Longarm grinned. "Which I notice that you haven't, but reckon I'll give it to you anyhow."

Billy spun around again to face his deputy. "Thank you for the vote of confidence." He smiled for the first time since Longarm had entered his office. "At least I think that is what that was."

"Ayuh, 'twas," Longarm said. "Now, are you gonna tell me about this here deal or not?"

Chapter 4

Longarm crossed Cherry Creek to his rooming house and collected the carpetbag he always kept packed and ready for the travel a deputy marshal had to endure. He paid his landlady the month's rent and took a hansom cab to the railroad station.

After so much time on the job Longarm pretty much knew the train schedules, but he checked the board of arrivals and departures anyway to make sure he was correct.

He was. The train he needed would be leaving in a little more than a half hour, so he settled down on a bench on the platform to wait. He passed the time playing peekaboo with a baby—a year old or so, he guessed—whose mother was an amazingly fat and ugly female. To the point that he was surprised she had managed to find herself someone to marry.

But the baby was cute.

Once on the train Longarm deposited his bag in an overhead rack, then went back to the smoker car and lighted a cheroot.

There he found a few like-minded gentlemen who wanted to relax with a friendly, low-stakes poker game.

He considered himself fortunate that he was only down

a dollar or so by the time the train pulled into Colorado Springs.

He went forward in the short string of cars to play one more game of peekaboo and retrieve his carpetbag. He waited for the passenger car to empty of the other disembarking passengers, then lighted another cheroot and stepped down onto the Denver & Rio Grande platform.

The fat woman with the baby was met by a husky, good-looking man who quite obviously beamed with pride in his family. So who the hell was he to judge? Longarm mused. They looked happy. Contented with one another.

Longarm felt a momentary twinge of envy at what that couple had between them, but he shoved it aside and left the platform in search of a hansom to carry him over to Manitou, where he knew he could rent a horse that would stand up to the rigors of mountain travel.

Chapter 5

It would have been quicker and in some ways easier to take the rails up to Fairplay and rent a horse there, but Longarm did not like the quality of the mounts a man could find in the mountains. There was a simple and entirely reasonable reason for that: It was damned expensive to haul feed up from the plains, so the few rental horses in the high country were apt to be underfed and overworked. And very poor quality because of it.

Better, he thought, to hire a mount in the flatlands, where there was enough call for saddle animals to justify a livery keeping some good ones.

"You again, Long? What are you up to this time?"

"Hello, Charlie. How are you?" Longarm shook hands with the lanky, redheaded hostler and offered the man a cheroot.

Charlie winked and bit off a good third of the slender cigar. It was the man's habit to chew his tobacco rather than risk striking a match within the barn full of combustible hay and straw. "Thanks, Custis."

Longarm had known Charlie for years and liked him. But not enough to invite the man to call him Longarm.

"Will this be on a government voucher like usual?"

Longarm nodded. "Like usual, Charlie."

"Well, walk out back and take your pick. I'll step inside and start the paperwork."

"Any recommendations?"

The hostler grinned. "Yeah. *Don't* pick that wall-eyed red son of a bitch. He's strong, but every once in a while he'll go crazy and blow up for no reason at all. When he does that, I've never known a man who could stick with him."

Longarm tipped his hat back and laughed. "You know good an' well, Charlie, that you've just picked out the horse I'll be taking."

"Kinda figured that," Charlie said, working up a little tobacco juice and spitting. "Go ahead and fetch him in. And pick you a saddle that you like. I got four of them hanging over there. I see you aren't carrying your own this time out."

"Oh, I almost forgot. I'll need a second horse. Maybe not so strong but steady, something that'll go easy on the end of a lead rope. I'll have a prisoner packed on him an' be leading him instead o' letting this fella handle any reins."

"Got a short, fat pinto that will be perfect for that. Steady as an anvil. And about as smart as one too. Now, excuse me, Custis. I got to start my paperwork."

Longarm ambled through the barn to the corrals out back to bring in the two horses Charlie had recommended.

Chapter 6

The coach road up to South Park followed and occasionally splashed through a cold-water creek. Longarm had fished that stream a time or two in the past and had taken some fine trout from it. He rather wished he had time now to stop and fish a little, but that was out of the question. He had work to do. And Billy's back to protect.

He stopped short of the rim overlooking the wide, grassy expanse of South Park. Jagged mountain peaks could be seen in most directions that the eye could find, many of them white with last year's snowpack.

He dismounted and tethered both animals. You never knew how far you can trust a rented horse, and ground reining was for fools. Both horses had performed well on the ride up from Manitou. The sorrel had not blown up under him and the pinto was docile as a pup.

Once the horses were established on a patch of grass, Longarm dipped a pot of water from the creek and built a small fire to heat water for coffee. He kept a packet of travel rations composed of items that would not easily spoil: crushed coffee beans, flour, salt, sugar, lard, raisins, and jerky. If a man had those, he could not only survive, he could be comfortable while he did it.

While the coffee was boiling, he mixed a little dough and wrapped it around a stick, then held that over the fire, turning it, until his biscuit was done. The coffee was ready at about the same time. Between the dough, the jerky, and the coffee, he had a fine and entirely satisfying meal.

By that time it was near dark, the sun sinking down behind the sawtooth mountains to the west. He checked on the horses, drank the last of the coffee, and kicked dirt over his fire before settling down for the night.

He fell asleep almost instantly.

He was wakened just as suddenly.

And rudely.

The horses were going crazy. The sorrel was thrashing and kicking. The normally phlegmatic pinto was screaming and bucking.

Longarm sat up and blinked, tried to rub the sleep out of his eyes. At first he thought the horses were fighting with each other. Then he saw that there was a dark, shadowy shape just beyond the horses. This dark mass seemed to be the focus of their attention.

The sorrel squealed and lashed out at the thing with its hind hoofs. It whirled, reared up, and tried to strike with its forefeet, but only succeeded in becoming entangled in the rope Longarm had used to tether it with. The sorrel fell heavily onto its side.

Unlike the sorrel's attempts to fight, the pinto was intent on trying to escape. It had run to the end of its tether and now stood trembling, feet braced wide apart, with its butt toward the menace.

With only starlight and a quarter moon to give light, Longarm could not see for sure what the intruder was. Either a bear or a panther, he guessed. Either might be found here. Either might have a taste for horseflesh.

Either was apt to be shy of humans though.

Longarm grabbed up his .45. And wished he had brought

a rifle along. Or at the least had a blazing fire where he could snatch up a firebrand. Still, the .45 was what he had and so that was what he could use.

He ran to the sorrel. The horse was struggling to regain its feet, but the bear—it was a large black bear, probably a sow with cubs to feed—had its teeth sunk into the horse's off hindquarter.

Longarm ran up to the fighting pair and snapped a shot off, aiming deliberately just a little high so as to avoid hitting the horse.

His bullet grazed the top of the bear's scalp. It was not a killing shot, but it annoyed the bruin so that it let go its hold on the sorrel. The horse scrambled to its feet and began furiously kicking the bear, which tumbled backward, rolling over and over in a ball of fur.

The sorrel tried to follow in a counterattack but was drawn up short by the tether.

Longarm fired again, a spear of fire streaking toward the bear. He was pretty sure he hit the bear in the body, although he was almost positive it would not be a killing shot. It would take more than one hastily aimed .45 slug to be that.

And anyway he had no real desire to kill the woolly creature, only to scare it away and protect the horses.

The bear howled, snarling and snapping its jaws. Then it dropped to all fours and turned away, loping back into the brush on the north side of the coach road.

Longarm shoved the Colt into his waistband and returned to his blankets to find his boots and pull them on. Then he picked up the packet of lard from his traveling supplies and went to calm the nervous horses and to doctor the sorrel's bite wounds as best he could.

A glance toward the stars told him he had only been asleep a few hours. It was much too late—or too early, depending on how one wanted to look at it—to get up now. Besides, the horses needed time to calm down before he headed out again.

He took care of the sorrel as best he could with the lard, then went back to bed.

He kept the Colt clutched in his hand while he slept, though, just in case the bear returned.

Chapter 7

Daybreak allowed Longarm to assess the damage that had been done to the sorrel. The bear attack had left puncture wounds on the right ham, but the beast had not had time to use its claws or to rip chunks of meat out of the horse.

The punctures had bled copiously, but they were already crusted over with dried blood. Longarm led the sorrel over to the creek and bathed the leg, washing the dried blood away and, more important, cooling the injured leg.

The sorrel walked with a limp, favoring the off hind, but the walking seemed to loosen the leg and allow the horse to more easily move. Longarm thought—hoped—it would be all right under saddle if he did not push it very hard.

As for the pinto, it was grazing calmly and acting as if nothing had ever happened. It seemed to have completely forgotten the bear attack.

Longarm took his time about breaking camp so as to give the sorrel more time for the pain to ease and for any swelling to subside. He rebuilt his fire and made another pot of coffee, something he rarely did in the morning when he was on the trail.

He had a light breakfast of jerky and a handful of raisins, all washed down with the hot coffee.

He waved to a passing stagecoach bound for the diggings at Fairplay or perhaps passing through the Bayou Salade and down Trout Creek Pass to Buena Vista and on to Leadville. The coach was full to the point that there were three passengers riding with the luggage on the roof. They seemed in good enough spirits; everyone returned his wave with friendly gestures of their own.

Finally, about mid-morning, he saddled both horses and climbed onto the sorrel.

And instantly came off again.

The animal had gone into a frenzy of bucking and kicking and snorting to the point that Longarm damn near regretted saving the animal from that bear attack.

He hit the ground hard, rolled, and grabbed for the reins he had dropped, more out of surprise than anything else.

He managed to get hold of one rein and held tight on to it while he brought the sorrel's head back down where it belonged.

The horse wheeled and tried to kick him. Longarm stepped in too close for the horse to get any leverage. He kicked it in the belly, which seemed to surprise the sorrel. Longarm knew good and well he had not hurt the horse, but his response did startle it.

It dropped to all fours and turned its head, one wide eye peering at him.

Charlie had said something about it going crazy, he remembered now. The horse had behaved perfectly all day yesterday. Longarm just hoped it had gotten its insanity out of its system for today now.

"All right, damn you. Let's see how this goes 'cause I'd hate t' have to shoot you an' put the government on the hook t' pay for you."

He retrieved the pinto's lead rope and rather gingerly climbed back onto the sorrel.

The horse acted like nothing had ever happened or would happen again.

"All right, dammit," Longarm muttered as he reined his sorrel north into the rugged country south of the old ghost town of Bailey.

The pinto followed, docile as a beagle pup.

Chapter 8

Shortly after noon Longarm reached an abandoned settlement. The log cabins, cobbled together out of locally available wood like pine and aspen—neither one of which was particularly well suited to building—stood mute and gray and empty.

TARRYALL, a crooked, hand-lettered sign announced. It did not much look like the sort of place where a man would want to tarry.

Judging by the buildings that were left behind, Tarryall had had a population of several dozen, no more. It had not lasted long, as there was still wood left standing, wood that would have been cut for firewood had the town existed very long.

Probably, he guessed, it grew up around some placer diggings in the adjacent stream.

By then the sorrel was limping badly, and Longarm required not much by way of an excuse to pull it in for the night.

He first rode the horses over to the creek and let them water, then rigged a hitch rope between two young pines. He tied the horses and unloaded them. He was busy collecting dry, age-gray shingles off the back of a nearby shed, figuring to use them for a quick-burning, almost smokeless fire for his nooning.

"Hey! What the hell do you think you're doing?"

Longarm spun around, his right hand automatically leaping to the butt of his Colt at the unexpected challenge.

A woman stood beside the front corner of one of the rickety cabins.

Her age was indeterminate. So was her shape. She was as dry and age-grayed as the shingles he held cradled in one arm. Her hair was done up in a loose bun, and her dress was a gray and shapeless drape that covered her from head to toe.

"I asked what the hell you're doing," she demanded.

"I'm just a traveler," Longarm said. "My horse was bit in the leg by a bear last night. I'm stopping here to give him some rest."

"Bear bite? Damn!" the woman snapped. "Let me see."

Longarm backed away and motioned toward the sorrel.

The woman hurried between the two cabins where Longarm had stopped. She walked around behind both animals, looking them over quickly before seizing on the sorrel as the one with the problem.

She moved closer and dropped to her knees behind the afflicted leg. If she worried that the sometimes spooky horse might kick her, she certainly did not show it.

She reached up and gently touched the wounded ham, then briskly stood with a loud grunt of effort.

"I can fix that," she declared. "Give me just one minute. I'll be right back."

The woman hustled away, disappearing toward the front of the cabins. She was gone probably less than a minute before she returned with a small pot of some black, sticky, vile-smelling concoction. Tar, he suspected, with a number of other ingredients stirred in as well.

She used the flat of a split stick to daub the stinking stuff onto the puncture wounds. Once she had done that, she looked up at Longarm like he had committed some sort of sin. She stood and wagged a scolding finger at him.

"You, young man, could have ruined this fine animal. Now, just you let Lettie fix him up. Let him stand for one full day. By evening tomorrow he should be fine as new."

"What did . . ."

"Never you mind what I did. What I did was to doctor him, and he was in need of it, no thanks to you. Now carry your traps into that cabin there. It isn't being used by anybody right now. Go on. On with you." She made a motion as if sweeping him away. "This animal will be fine as rain, but you mind what I say."

"Yes, ma'am," Longarm said obediently, suppressing an urge to laugh at Lettie's seriousness. He picked up his things and began transferring them into the cabin as he had been instructed.

Chapter 9

Longarm woke up fairly early that evening. He was not sure of the time, but he knew he had not yet had enough sleep.

He awoke realizing that he had a raging hard-on. That was not particularly unusual, but this time it was caused by moist heat being applied to his cock, making it stand tall as a tent pole.

"What the . . . ?"

"Just you lie down, mister, and let Lettie."

He turned cold, but the fat old woman had him by the cods—literally—and was busy rubbing him up and down.

As his eyes adjusted to the dimness, Longarm could see that Lettie was naked. It was a sight he would rather not have seen.

Her dugs were enormous, heavily veined bags that hung over a distended belly.

That was bad enough, but she also had an apron of fat that hung almost to her knees. She had to lift it to get it out of the way. She deposited it, warm and soft and heavy, on Longarm's belly so as to give herself access to a hairy nest.

Lettie had not bathed recently, as he could tell once the apron of fat was pulled out of the way. Her pussy stank, plain and simple.

Longarm wrinkled his nose and tried to roll away, but Lettie had her fat, dimpled knees firmly planted on either side of his body. She held him trapped in place beneath the weight of her.

She lifted her apron of fat and shifted it a little, then reached down and took hold of his cock to guide it into place.

Longarm shuddered. He did not know how to dissuade her by any means short of grabbing his .45 and shooting her in the gut.

He was tempted to do exactly that.

In the end all he could manage to do was to close his eyes and pretend it was someone else—almost anyone else—who was so vigorously fucking him.

He lay there, submitting, while Lettie's slippery, smelly pussy jumped up and down on his cock.

She fucked him like that for several minutes—it seemed longer—then grunted loudly as she reached some sort of climax. After she did that she let herself down onto him, her fat engulfing Longarm's slender, muscular body like a bowl of warm gelatin.

He hated this woman's touch. Hated her smell. Hated what had just happened to him here.

Lettie picked herself up and waddled naked out of the cabin, leaving Longarm to wonder just what in hell had happened here.

He went back to sleep and by morning had convinced himself—almost convinced himself—that the whole thing had been a bad dream.

Even so he hurriedly saddled his horses, rolled up the hitch rope, and got the hell out of there.

Chapter 10

Curen Town, Billy had said. Longarm found it easily enough by striking off on a road that ran generally northwest to southeast and following it into the surrounding mountains.

The town was small but seemed to be prosperous enough. It had a sawmill and, as a consequence, buildings made of lumber rather than logs. The livery, such as it was, held only burros and a few small mules.

"How much to board these horses overnight?" Longarm asked the lean, gray-haired man who was running the place.

"Two dollars a night," the hostler said.

"That seems a mite dear," Longarm complained.

The hostler shrugged. "Two dollars." He grinned. "Each. Take it or leave it. And by the bye, that's for grass hay. No grain."

"Will you take a government voucher?" Longarm asked.

"Sure. You want grain? Oats is fifty cents more. Each."

"No grain. Grass hay will be good enough. So four dollars it is." Longarm turned the horses over to him. "Where can a man get a room for the night?"

It was too late in the day to find his prisoner and head back down this evening. Better to get an early start in the morning, he thought. He followed the hostler's directions to a hotel and checked in.

His room was tidy enough. The mattress sagged but only a little, and the sheets were fresh. They should be. The place charged five dollars a night.

"I'll want a bath later," he told the desk clerk when he came back downstairs.

"Sorry. No bath here, but the barber has a tub and hot water. He'll charge you a quarter if you have your own soap, thirty cents to use his."

"All right, thanks."

There would be time enough later for that, Longarm thought. First he wanted to check in with the town marshal. Billy had said the prisoner was already in custody, so in the morning all he had to do was to retrieve the horses, collect the man, and leave. That should certainly be easy enough.

He got directions to the jail, the barbershop, and to a good café, thanked the clerk and headed out.

The town marshal first, he decided, turning in that direction.

He walked past a post office. Not just some postal drop inside a general store but a freestanding post office building of its own, he saw. Interesting. It was obvious from this whole town that the founder, Edward Curen, was a man of wealth and taste and influence. Especially influence. It took plenty of that for any town to have a freestanding post office, much less for such a small town. No wonder Billy felt a little insecure in his job right now. After all, the attorney general could replace him with the stroke of a pen, and both Billy Vail and Edward Curen knew it.

No one was in at the marshal's office, so Longarm went next door to ask after the man.

"You'll find Seth over at Ed Curen's office, I think. This is about the time they usually have their meetings."

"Meetings?" Longarm asked.

The storekeeper only shrugged and went back to tidying his shelves.

Longarm returned to the marshal's office and again went inside. There was no marshal present. More interesting, there was no prisoner in the lone jail cell. The cell door stood open, the key protruding from the heavy lock.

"What the hell is going on here?" Longarm asked of no one in the empty room.

No one answered him.

Chapter 11

Longarm went back to the storekeeper for a better explanation of what meetings he had been talking about, but all he got this time was a shake of the man's head and a muted "I don't know 'bout such things" in return. Then the man ducked his head and began sweeping the floor as if his very life depended on it.

If he could not find the town marshal at the moment, he could ask again at the café, Longarm decided, and fill his belly at the same time.

The Wonder Café was only a block away. Longarm walked over there and helped himself to a seat at the counter. There were three others already at the counter and a dozen or so patrons seated at the handful of tables jammed into the place.

"Wonder," Longarm said when a gent in an apron came to take his order. "What makes this place such a wonder?"

The waiter grunted and said, "I do. I'm Sam Wonder."

Longarm laughed and said, "That does explain things, doesn't it. Well then, Mr. Wonder, what would you recommend to a hungry man? Whatever it is, just bring me some of it. No, make that a lot of it 'cause I'm hungry enough to eat most anything that doesn't eat me first."

"Sit back and undo your belt then, neighbor. You'll be groaning when you walk out of here, I guarantee it," Sam Wonder said.

"While you're contemplating what to feed me," Longarm said, "you might suggest where I could find the marshal."

"That's easy. Him and the town fathers will be in their meeting about now, but they should be done in an hour or so," Wonder said.

"In that case, you can quit bringing me food in about one hour," Longarm said, smiling.

"I'll make a note of that," Wonder said. The man turned to his grill and in short order produced a huge slab of roasted meat—elk, Longarm thought—with all the fixings.

"Now this," Longarm said, "is a meal fit for a king."

"I cannot disagree," Wonder said with a smile.

Longarm grabbed the knife and fork that were offered and dug in to the elbows.

As Longarm was finishing his meal, Wonder came over to his end of the counter and said, "You were asking about Marshal Seth?"

Longarm looked up. "Yes, why?"

"'Cause that's him coming through the door just now," Wonder said, inclining his head in the direction of a pair of men on their way into the café. "He's the one in the calfskin vest."

"Thanks, Sam." Longarm swung around on his stool and stood up, rising to greet the two.

Chapter 12

Seth Greenwald was short and something on the squat side as men went. He was dressed in a broadcloth suit and wore a heavy gold chain stretched across the front of his calfskin vest. He wore a black derby hat and yellow spats. A rather large and very shiny badge was pinned to the breast pocket of his suit coat.

Longarm got one look at the impeccably groomed dandy and took an instant dislike to the man.

He conceded that he had known some fine lawmen who happened also to dress like gamblers or dandies. Masterson came to mind in that category. But he seriously doubted that Seth Greenwald was a man to compare with Bat.

Longarm drank the last of the coffee in his mug and watched while Greenwald and his equally dandy companion chose a corner table and seated themselves, then Longarm swung around on the counter stool and stood. He strode over to Greenwald's table and stopped close beside it.

Greenwald looked up, annoyance tugging down the corners of his mouth.

"This is a private conversation," he snapped.

Longarm ignored the comment and said, "You're what passes for law in this town?"

"I told you, dammit, this is a private conversation. Now, get away from me before I put you in handcuffs and run you in."

Longarm threw his head back and laughed. "You and who the hell else, you miserable piece of dog-shit of an excuse for a lawman."

"Why I . . . I . . ." Greenwald blustered. "Me and my, uh, my deputies . . ."

"Oh, bullshit," Longarm cut in. "You got no deputies. You also got no business pretending to be a marshal except it gives you an excuse to strut around with your chest stuck out thinking you can lord it over people that are better'n you."

"You can't talk to me like that. Why, I'll have you thrown in jail so quick it will make you dizzy," Greenwald declared. But the town marshal did not stand up from his table—he would have found himself a good head shorter than Longarm had he done so—and he made no move to carry out the threat.

"Where's your prisoner?" Longarm returned.

"What?"

"Your prisoner," Longarm said. "You remember about them, don't you? You're s'posed to have a man name of Curen in jail here waitin' to be transported down to Denver for arraignment and trial on charges of tampering with the mail. Well, I been over to your jail. It's empty. So where is your prisoner?"

"You . . . Who do you think you are?" Greenwald asked, it seeming finally to dawn on him that this man in front of him was no citizen with a petty complaint to lodge.

"I think I'm a deputy United States marshal," Longarm said, "here to take custody of that prisoner and do the transporting. So I will ask you again . . . *Marshal* . . . one more time before I put *you* in cuffs and charge you with obstruction of justice . . . Where is the prisoner?"

"I . . . uh . . . I . . ."

The other man at Greenwald's table gave Longarm a level

look and calmly said, "The so-called prisoner has been released on bail."

"Ain't no so-called about it," Longarm said. "And who are you?"

The man rose and leaned across the table with an extended hand to shake. He said, "I'm Lester Wilson. Call me Les. I am counsel for the town."

"You're a lawyer," Longarm said.

Wilson nodded. "I am, sir."

Longarm accepted the man's hand and shook it. "Custis Long," he said to introduce himself.

"A pleasure," Wilson responded.

Longarm grinned. "Why is it that I doubt that, Mr. Wilson?"

"Perhaps," Wilson said, "but I am sure we can reach an amicable, um, accommodation concerning the younger Mr. Curen. Please. Sit down. Join us. We can work something out."

Chapter 13

Longarm took the chair that was offered, but he said, "The only accommodation I'm lookin' for is to take the man into custody and take him down to Denver with me. And since you are representing the town, and presumably this bag o' crap along with it, you might want tell your client to present Edward Curen, Jr., to me before I misunderstand and slap him in cuffs along with Curen."

"Oh, come now, Mr. Long. It needn't be as black-and-white as that. Would you like some coffee? Something harder, perhaps?"

"Mr. Wilson, this deal is more black-and-white than you seem to think," Longarm insisted.

Wilson grunted. Greenwald looked away as if this conversation had nothing to do with him. "Let me ask you something, Deputy. Have you met Ed yet?"

"No, sir, I have not, though meeting him is the whole reason why I came up here."

Wilson motioned with an upraised finger and the waiter was instantly at their table. "Yes, Mr. Wilson? Is there something more you require?"

"Two things, Jensen. Deputy Long will have a cup of coffee." As an aside to Longarm, Wilson said, "You can drink that while Seth and I have our meal." Then back to the waiter he added, "And from now on, anything Deputy Long would care for is on the house to him. The town will pay for it." He smiled. "You can tell Sam I said it's all right."

"Yes, sir, Mr. Wilson." The waiter practically saluted—or wagged his tail—in an effort to please the lawyer, who obviously had considerable influence in Curen Town.

The young man was gone in a flash and back again moments later with a cup of steaming coffee that he set in front of Longarm, never mind that Longarm did not want to accept anything from these people. Anything, that is, except Edward Curen, Jr.

It would have been churlish, Longarm figured, for him to reject something as inconsequential as a lousy cup of coffee. And the fact is, the coffee was not lousy. If anything it was as superior as Sam Wonder's cooking was. But a nickel cup of coffee could not be considered a bribe. He already was beginning to suspect that genial Les Wilson was the sort who would hit a man with any club that came to hand, with no regard for Marquis of Queensbury rules.

"Good coffee," he said over the rim of his mug.

Chapter 14

Longarm waited, politely drinking coffee while the two local dandies ate a heavy supper, then Wilson said, "If you would like to meet Curen now, Marshal, we can take you to him."

"I would, indeed. It's what I came here for, y'know."

The lawyer laid down a five-dollar coin to pay for what were at best a pair of dollar dinners—and likely half that much—and dropped his napkin on top of the payment. "Ready, Long?"

Longarm nodded, standing and retrieving the Stetson he had left on the counter beside the stool he'd occupied earlier.

"Are you coming, Seth?" Wilson asked his dinner companion.

"No, I don't think so, Les."

"Suit yourself." To Longarm, Wilson said, "Come along then. I will introduce you."

"Right behind you."

Wilson led the way to a tall, narrow building constructed of kiln-fired red brick. It must have cost a fortune and a barrel full of sweat, human and animal alike, to get all that brick into Curen Town, but then obviously Edward Curen,

Sr., had it to spend. And wanted everyone to know that he did.

Longarm had not ever met the man and already did not like him.

He would say one thing for Curen though. The front door to his building opened directly into his office, and Curen did not feel any need to keep bodyguards close at hand. The man himself was behind the desk situated directly in front of the doors.

Edward Curen, Sr., was smaller than Longarm had expected. He was slender, with blond hair and side whiskers. He wore a boiled shirt with a celluloid collar attached, a string tie, and dark oversleeves. The tie had a keeper mounted in it, with one of the largest gold nuggets Longarm had ever seen. And he had seen a great many gold nuggets—other people's nuggets, that is—in his day.

When Longarm and Lester Wilson entered the large and rather lavishly appointed office, Curen stood, stripped off the sleeve protectors, and extended his hand.

"You would be Deputy Long, I presume," the town boss said, smiling. "May I call you Longarm?"

Curen read Longarm's surprised expression. He laughed and said, "No, you haven't introduced yourself to anyone here in Curen Town by that name, Deputy, but I make it my business to know what is happening here and who is doing it. May I say that you have a good reputation. You are said to be honest and fair but willing to listen to reason. You won't break the law, but you will bend the hell out of it when the occasion arises. Oh, forgive me. I've forgotten my manners. Sit down, please. Over there."

Curen pointed to an overstuffed sofa with blue flocked-velvet upholstery. He himself took a matching Queen Anne armchair that sat facing the sofa.

It amused Longarm to notice that the seat of the sofa was a good four inches lower than that of the armchair—which gave Curen a position superior to that of his guests. Deliberate, of course. He wondered if the boss thought he was being subtle there.

Even so, Longarm's greater height—six feet plus to Curen's five-foot-seven or -eight—put them at each other's eye level when they sat.

Curen apparently did not like that because moments after sitting, he bounced to his feet and began pacing slowly back and forth in front of the sofa.

"I understand why you are here, Longarm. Of course I do. But you should understand that, well, boys will be boys. Have you been filled in on the particulars of the, um, the charges?"

"In general," Longarm said, peering up at Curen while the man continued to pace.

Curen paused his pacing long enough to take up a small bell that rested on his desk. He rang it, and instantly a back door opened and a man wearing black trousers and a black satin waistcoat stepped into the room.

"Rye whiskey for our guest, Charles, and a brandy for me. Lester, what will you have?"

"Brandy, thank you," Wilson said.

Longarm intended to refuse the offer, but the waiter or butler or whatever he was disappeared as quickly as he had come.

"Where was I?" Curen said. "Oh, yes. This foolishness about theft from the mails. It was really nothing of the sort, you understand. Eddie simply intercepted a note sent by a rival in a, um, a matter of the heart. That is all this was about. Surely you have been young and in love, Longarm. Eddie was. Still is. He, um, was overcome with passion. He acted rashly. He regrets that decision now, of course. It will not happen again." Curen smiled, but the expression failed to reach his eyes. "I can assure you of that. Eddie has learned his lesson."

"I'm glad to hear that, Mr. Curen. Now Edward . . . Eddie, if you prefer . . . can come with me down to Denver and straighten the whole thing out with the judge. Then he'll be free to come back here as he pleases."

"Yes, well, I cannot allow that, Longarm. I'm sorry, but I really can't."

Charles returned carrying a tray with the requested drinks. Longarm ignored his. Accepting a cup of coffee from Lester Wilson was one thing. Taking whiskey from this man who wanted Billy Vail's job seemed like something that would be repugnant. It would have the feel of being disloyal to Billy, and Longarm wanted no part of that or anything that smacked of it.

He did not make an issue of refusing the drink. He just let Charles set it down and then ignored it. Both Curen and Wilson sipped from their golden brandies. "Excellent, Ed. Simply excellent," Wilson commented. Longarm did not doubt the truth of the statement. Ed Curen seemed like a man who wanted only the best of everything.

"I want you to meet Eddie, Longarm. Would tomorrow morning be convenient for you?"

"Sure, Ed, that'd be fine by me."

"Over breakfast, shall we say? At eight?"

"Eight o'clock would be fine."

"Good. I'll send someone for you about a quarter to."

Longarm nodded and stood, understanding that this meeting was over. Wilson remained seated.

Curen moved forward, obviously intending to offer his hand again, but Longarm pretended not to see as he turned and got the hell out of the great man's presence.

Chapter 15

Longarm got out of there with the feeling that he needed a bath. Or a drink. Or both. He stepped into the first saloon he came to and stood at the bar.

"What will it be, sir?" the barman asked.

"Rye whiskey," Longarm told him. He was sure the bar whiskey would not be anywhere close to the quality of the rye Ed Curen served, but this rye would have no implied strings attached.

He paid for his own whiskey, by damn, or traded drinks with friends. But Custis Long could not be bought. It was a point of pride.

Not that he thought Curen believed he was for sale for a glass of rye whiskey, but he suspected that simple glass of whiskey might open the door—at least in Curen's mind—to other forms of bribery. Subtle or outright but bribery nonetheless.

The man wanted to "negotiate." Except there would be no negotiation. There would only be duty observed. Duty performed. That was the way Billy Vail ran things. If Ed Curen somehow managed to replace Billy, he could run the office on his terms. Until then, Longarm would handle things in a way that Billy would approve.

And if Curen was appointed United States marshal for the Denver district, Longarm would be looking for work elsewhere. He had no intention of working for Ed Curen. Ever. In any capacity or for any amount of money.

"Another?"

Longarm snapped out of his thoughts about Billy and Curen and such and returned to the here and now, half surprised to find himself with an empty glass on the bar in front of him. "Oh, uh, yeah. Another."

The barman poured and Longarm paid. He owed no one in this town a single thing, and he intended to keep it that way.

"And another," he said, tossing the rye back.

The whiskey was harsh and of poor quality. The nice thing about bad whiskey was that it became better and better the more a man drank it.

"Another," he said, laying a tiny, gold quarter eagle down.

Chapter 16

Longarm stumbled and cussed and swayed just a little as he made his way up to his room. He cussed a little more about the third time he tried to get the key into the lock, but he did manage eventually, got the door open, and walked inside.

He was mildly startled to find that his lamp had already been lighted, but he was much more surprised to discover that his bed was already occupied too.

"What, uh—Sorry, miss, I must've got the wrong room somehow, I . . ."

He took a step backward and turned his head to look at the room number on the door.

It was the right number, and this was his room. He could see his own much traveled carpetbag there where he had left it, and that was his slicker hanging on a hook, also where he had left it some hours earlier.

So who was the young woman lying in his bed with the covers pulled up to her chin?

"It's about time you got here," the girl said. "I've been waiting for hours and hours."

"If I had known that, I'd've come sooner," he drawled.

"But if you don't mind me askin', who the hell are you and what're you doing here? Other than waitin' for me, that is."

By way of an answer she swept the covers aside.

She was naked as a boiled egg. And looked much more edible.

The girl was uncommonly good-looking, with jet-black hair that fell in curls above a button nose, small chin and mouth, ripe lips, and eyes that were . . . He was not sure what color her eyes were. One moment they seemed to be blue, the next violet. For sure those eyes were large and lovely and mesmerizing.

Her waist was tiny, narrow enough to make Longarm suspect she was from the Deep South and had had a lower rib removed so she could cinch her waist down smaller than nature ever intended.

Her tits were not especially large, but the contrast with her waist made them seem so. They were firm and pointed, tipped with pale pink nipples that stood tall.

Her pussy hair was only lightly curled. It looked to be soft. Bright red cunt lips winked out from within that nest of black hair.

Her legs were slender, not overly long but well shaped.

All in all she was a girl who could excite a man's passions. Longarm's passions were damn sure excited. And then some. His pecker felt like it would burst the buttons of his fly.

"You, uh, you say you been waiting for me?" he said.

She smiled. The smile made her even prettier. Her teeth were small and white and even. "I have," she said. "I've been wanting to meet you."

"I'd say this is the nicest introduction I ever had," Longarm said with a grin. He closed the door behind him and asked, "Should I lock it?"

"Please do," the girl said, giggling.

He shot the bolt closed to lock the door and turned back to the naked girl in his bed.

"Why don't you take your clothes off and join me?" she offered, smiling.

"I thought you'd never ask," Longarm said with a grin, as he began to unbutton and strip.

Chapter 17

"Oh, oh . . . yes. Harder now. Harder. Now soft and slow. Ah! Wonderful. I'm . . . I'm . . . I'm coming now."

She did not need to make that last announcement. Longarm could damn sure tell that from the way her hips bucked and thrashed and from the way her thighs clamped hard around his ears.

When she subsided, limp and languid, Longarm sat up and wiped the pussy juice off his chin. The girl did taste uncommonly good, he had to admit. She was clean and fresh and had splashed some sort of lavender scent down there. All in all not a bad pussy to lick, and this girl reached her shuddering climax fairly quickly.

"Mind if I smoke a little before we get down to serious business here?" he asked.

"Can I have one too?" she responded, sitting up in his bed.

Longarm retrieved his coat and took out a single cheroot. He nipped the twist off the end, found a match in a pocket of his discarded vest, and lighted the slender cigar. The two of them sat side by side on the side of the bed and shared the cheroot back and forth between them for several minutes in companionable silence.

Then Longarm said, "Mind if I ask you something?"

"You can ask me anything," she said, giggling. "I may even tell you the truth." The giggle turned into a laugh. "Or not."

"Well, what I'm wonderin'," he said, "is who the hell you are."

Her laughter deepened. Finally she said, "My name is Rebecca Thorn. I'm the girl Eddie is addicted to."

Longarm raised an eyebrow.

Rebecca added, "Poor Eddie was raised to be the son of a man who has high political aspirations. Ed Senior thinks people will judge him by his family as well as everything else." She shrugged. "I wouldn't know about such things. Maybe they will. The point is that Eddie hasn't ever had a chance to sow his wild oats." She laughed again.

"And believe me, Eddie has some wild oats to sow. To tell you the truth he isn't a very good fuck. Which I'm sure you will turn out to be. But, oh my, he does love it. He's like a big old puppy dog, panting around and doing whatever he thinks will get me to drop my drawers for him."

"If that's what you think of him," Longarm asked, handing the cheroot back to the girl, "why do you let him fuck you?"

She took a drag on the smoke and handed it back. "Because Edward Curen, Jr., would be a wonderfully good catch, that's why. Eddie would be my ticket to the good life. Wherever Ed Senior goes, young Eddie will be taken along. And I want a good life. A life with some money in it." She shuddered. "Not like . . . what I've always had before."

"You grew up poor?" he asked.

Rebecca nodded. "As a church mouse. And I didn't much like it."

"What makes you think Ed Senior will let his little boy marry a girl . . . forgive me for saying it, but a girl like you?"

She grinned. "Oh, I think he will. Just as soon as I get pregnant."

Longarm's eyebrows went up again.

Rebecca laughed. "No, I'm not knocked up yet, but I'm working on it. Hell, with any kind of luck you'll plant your flag in my belly after we finish this cigar."

"What good would that do you?" he asked.

"Look, Marshal, once I have a kid in my belly, who's to say who the daddy is. It will be whoever I say it is. And believe me, I will swear that the kid belongs to Eddie."

"You want a child?"

She shrugged. "I want to get married to Eddie. And I want everything that comes with that. I've had plenty of practice riding herd on snot-nose kids, back home with my brother and my sisters, and if I get bored with that and want to have some fun, Eddie and me will be able to afford to hire a nanny. It will be great, believe me. And I will be a *good* wife to him. I know how to dress and to speak. I've studied this stuff. I can make him proud of me in the parlor and screw his ears off in the bedroom. What more could any boy want?"

Longarm rubbed his ears and said, "Speaking of which, I think you damn near ripped my ears off just now."

Rebecca laughed. "Sorry. I guess I do get a little carried away when I cum."

"A little?" Longarm said.

"Mm, okay, maybe a lot." She crushed the cheroot out in an empty snuff tin on the bedside table and said, "Thinking of which, you've got me all horny and wet, sitting here seeing that tent pole you call a dick. I want to feel it inside me now. Would you mind?"

"Oh, I reckon I could stand it," Longarm drawled.

"Just promise me one thing, sweetie. Promise you'll cum inside me. No pulling out ahead of time."

"And if you get knocked up?"

She laughed again. "Then Eddie Curen, Jr., will be a daddy in about nine months. Now, come to me, sweetie," Rebecca said, lying back on his bed and spreading her legs wide.

"One thing," he said before reaching for her. "Why me? Why now?"

"Because I want you to promise you'll find a way to let Eddie stay here. Now that I have the pump primed, I don't want some bitch down in Denver getting her hooks into *my* future, that's why."

Longarm grunted, making no promises. To himself he thought pretty Rebecca was fixing to be mighty disappointed. A good screw was one thing, but duty was another. And never mind what Ed Senior wanted or what Rebecca Thorn would like. Eddie Curen was going down to Denver to stand trial. Period.

"Move over just a little bit, Becca. Move . . . Oh! Now, that, darlin', is just fine."

Chapter 18

As good as his word, Ed Curen's man knocked on Longarm's door promptly at a quarter to eight. Rebecca was long gone. She had slipped away around midnight. With or without a small package in her belly.

"Coming," Longarm called, pulling his coat on. He picked up his Stetson and adjusted it comfortably on his head, then by habit touched the butt of his revolver to make sure it was riding in its proper place on his belt. He grunted his satisfaction, then went to the door.

Curen's assistant, or courier, or whatever, was a young man with dark blond hair falling down over his forehead, half a dozen or so acne pimples surrounding his mouth, and brown eyes. He wore a suit, and if he carried a pistol or any other sort of weapon, Longarm could not spot it.

"Are you Eddie?" Longarm asked as he pulled his door closed and locked it—although what good the lock would do he did not know; certainly Rebecca had had no trouble getting in ahead of him.

"No, sir. My name is Anthony. I work for Mr. Curen."

"All right, Anthony. Where are we going and what are we going to do there?"

Anthony smiled. "Just follow me, sir."

Edward Curen surprised him. Anthony led him not to some fancy restaurant or to Curen's office building, but beyond the edge of town to a grove of young aspen surrounding a secluded bower. A table had been created with rough planks. Stools were set beside the table—four of them, Longarm noticed—and a wicker picnic basket sat in the middle.

Ed Curen, Sr., and Lester Wilson occupied two of the stools. Two were empty.

"Here you go, sir," Anthony said. He nodded pleasantly enough, then turned and slipped away into the shimmering aspen.

"Good morning, Long. I trust you slept well," Curen said.

"Passable," Longarm responded. "Where's Eddie?"

"In good time, please. Can't we relax and be civil for a few moments? Our business can wait until we eat."

"If you please," Longarm said.

Curen must have signaled somehow, because as soon as Longarm seated himself, the waiter from the previous evening, Jensen, appeared. Jensen opened the basket and handed around sandwiches made of thick and tasty rye bread with fried egg and ham between the slices.

There was also a carafe of strong coffee complete with all the fixings.

Longarm surrounded his breakfast and waited patiently for the other two to eat as well. Curen and Wilson spoke in low tones that Longarm did not bother to try to overhear. He sipped the coffee and let Curen take the lead, something the man was obviously intent on doing anyway.

When he was done eating, but not waiting for the lawyer to finish, Curen stood and brushed crumbs from his vest, then sat down again. He leaned forward and earnestly said, "We need to talk, Longarm."

"What we need," Longarm said, "is for you to produce Eddie so I can take him with me down to Denver. I can promise you he won't be harmed in any way. I will take good care of him. Once we get there, he'll be booked into the jail. Then he'll be arraigned. That won't take much time. A day or two at the most. Bail will be set. Soon as you post that, he'll be released. He can come back home in hardly no time at all. A trial date will be set some time in, oh, a month or two." Longarm smiled. "I suspect you will provide him with competent counsel for his defense. And that will be all there'll be to it."

Wilson nodded. "Just like I told you, Ed."

"Is there nothing I can say or, um, *do* to make you change your mind, Long?" Curen asked, emphasizing "do." It was clear enough that the man would pay a hefty bribe if Longarm asked for one. But no actual offer had been made, so no law was actually broken.

And Curen had a witness to that effect.

Sharp, Longarm thought. But as shady as this aspen bower and then some.

God help this country if Edward Curen ever got that appointment as United States marshal.

In fact Longarm wondered exactly why the man was aiming for that particular office.

He had something illegal that he needed to hide? Something that Billy or one of the attorney general's people were likely to discover if Curen was not in that office so he could block an investigation?

Or perhaps Curen merely wanted to use Billy's office as a stepping-stone to something higher.

Either way, Longarm sincerely hoped that Edward Curen never received that appointment. Never. Ever.

"I'm sorry, Mr. Curen, but the law must be observed. And that means I have to take Eddie with me down to Denver."

Curen nodded. "All right." He motioned toward Wilson. "Les told me that would be your answer, but . . . as a father . . . I had to try." He smiled. "No hard feelings, I hope."

"No, sir. No hard feelings."

The man nodded again, and once more must have given

some signal, because moments later there was a rustling within the quaking aspen and a young man came forward beside Anthony.

"I'm ready, Marshal," the fellow said.

Eddie was taller than his father, with dark blond hair and a much darker complexion. He did not appear to be armed, but Longarm stood and gave him a quick once-over to make sure.

"The sooner we start, son, the sooner you'll be back home," Longarm said.

"I took the liberty of having your animals packed and made ready for you," Wilson said. "I was, um, sure of what your decision would be. Your room has been taken care of and your personal things loaded onto the bay horse. Eddie's things are on the paint. I hope that is correct."

"Exactly right," Longarm said. "Thank you."

The fact was that he was fairly well pissed off that some stranger had gone into his room and brought his things out. Lordy, why did they have keys to that room anyway?

He was sure every tiny thing would be there when he got back to Denver and unpacked. It was the idea of it that he hated.

Done was done, however, and there was no changing anything now.

"Come along, Eddie."

"You won't be putting me in handcuffs, Marshal?"

"Do I need to?"

The young man smiled. "No, sir, of course not."

"Then let's you an' me go. I'll get you back here quick as we can."

Chapter 19

Eddie eyed the pinto horse skeptically. "He doesn't kick, does he?"

"Hell yes, he'll kick," Longarm said. "Just don't get where he can nail you an' you'll be all right."

The boy kept a wary eye on the animal as he climbed into the saddle.

Longarm had intended to allow Eddie to follow along more or less free, but now he rigged the lead rope again, just as he had to lead the pinto on the way up here from Manitou.

He checked the sorrel's hindquarter and was pleased to see the bear bite rapidly healing. The crazy woman in Tarryall had employed her healing powers well. She was a strange one, though.

Once he was sure the sorrel was ready for some work, he stepped into the saddle and took up the lead rope to the pinto.

"Let's go to Denver, Eddie."

"Yes, sir."

Longarm had intended to go back the way he had come, by way of the South Park rim and on down to Manitou, then from Colorado Springs up to Denver.

But that was a longer route and the main reason for

taking it would be so he could return the horses to their proper owner.

Now, on the spur of the moment, he decided to take the quicker route out through Fairplay and down from there. Once he reached the rails, he could leave the horses with instruction that they be returned to Manitou—they would wind up there eventually or the U.S. government would be billed for their value, one way or the other—while he and his agreeable prisoner took the quick and easy way down by railroad train.

All in all, he thought, this assignment was not turning out to be very difficult.

And he had had the bonus of a night with the lovely Miss Rebecca Thorn. Hell, that was worth something right there.

A hint of a smile touched his lips as they put Curen Town behind them in the dips and folds of the Rockies.

Chapter 20

Longarm led their little caravan into Fairplay around four in the afternoon. It was a town he knew from previous visits. He headed immediately to the tall courthouse building that lay on the edge of town, a block off the main street.

"Hello, Marshal," the on-duty deputy said with a smile as Longarm and his prisoner climbed the stairs to the third floor and stepped into the jail section of the courthouse.

"Hello yourself, Tommy. Have you and that pretty lady of yours gotten yourselves hitched yet?"

Tommy Benton's expression sagged. "She has, Marshal. I haven't."

"Oh, shit. I'm sorry, Tommy. What happened?"

"She met a fancy man from down on the flatlands. He courted her with flowers while all I ever done was to take her fishing and like that." Benton sighed. "It was my own fault, Longarm. Now I know. Now that it's too late."

"I'm sorry, Tommy. I thought . . . Well, you know what I thought."

Benton shrugged. "I thought so too, Marshal. Anyway, that's all over and done with. What can I do for you now?"

Longarm motioned toward his prisoner. "I need to put this fella behind your bars overnight, if that's all right."

"You know it is. Have you seen the sheriff?"

"No, not yet."

"Don't worry about it. I'll take care of everything for you."

"Thanks, Tommy. You're a pal."

"Aw, I owe you more than I could ever repay already."

"You owe me nothing, but I'm happy for the friendship," Longarm said.

"You can put the man in the last cell there. I won't put nobody in there with him."

"Can you feed him for me too, Tommy?"

"Of course I can. The county will have to charge you twenty cents for his supper and fifteen for his breakfast. Is that all right?"

"Just fine, thanks," Longarm said. "What time do you get off tonight? Maybe you can join me for supper."

"Damn, I wish I could, but I'm on duty here until midnight."

"That'd be a mite late for supper an' early for breakfast, I think."

"Next time then," Tommy said.

"It's a deal."

Benton shepherded the prisoner into cell number four and closed the door on him. Longarm could not help but notice that the rawboned, dead-silent prisoner winced when the cell door clanked shut behind him.

"It's all right, kid," Longarm assured him. "Deputy Benton here will take good care of you."

"Promise?"

Longarm nodded. "It's a promise."

"Mine too," Tommy said.

"Your what?"

"My promise too."

"Oh, yeah. That."

When they walked out to the cubicle beside the staircase

to fill out the paperwork, Tommy said, "Not the sharpest chisel in the box, is he?"

"I'd have to agree," Longarm said. "Quiet too. Hasn't hardly said a word all day, so don't expect him to entertain you tonight."

"That's one thing about pulling jail duty. It isn't exactly good company most of the time."

Longarm grinned. "But you meet the most interesting people."

Tommy faked a scowl, then laughed. "What time will you be wanting him in the morning?"

"I'll check the stagecoach schedule and let you know later."

"Where are you going with him? There aren't so many coaches running through here. I might be able to tell you."

"We're headed down to Denver."

"By train?"

Longarm nodded.

"Be here by seven. The coach leaves a quarter past, and they're usually pretty prompt."

"All right, thanks."

"I'll have him fed and ready for you by then," Tommy assured him.

Longarm thanked the young deputy again and headed down the stairs. He needed to see to the horses, then get a hotel room. After that he would be free for the evening. He was looking forward to the off-duty time, Fairplay being one of his favorite towns in all of Colorado.

There was something about the place that he enjoyed. It was small but lively, and the people there tended to be hard-working and honest, unlike some of the sharps he ran into down in Denver.

First, though, he would see to the horses. Hopefully they could be sent back down to Manitou.

If nothing else, they could be tied on the back of a coach headed down that way.

After that supper and who knew what other sorts of pleasure he might run into in this delightful little town.

Chapter 21

Longarm yawned and leaned back from the card table. He did not like to count his money at the table, but he knew he was well ahead. He had started with four dollars in silver. Now he could see a five-dollar half eagle and two gold quarter eagles gleaming out from a tidy pile of silver. Not bad for an early evening's play.

"Gentlemen, I got t' quit. My belly is whining and cussing at me. Reckon it's time I get some grub."

"You can fetch a plate from the free lunch spread," one of the other players, a man named Stefan, suggested. Stefan obviously did not want that pile of money to leave the table before he had another shot at it. On the other hand, Longarm had seen Stefan play cards; he was probably better off to have Longarm leave now.

"Right, but I got something better'n that in mind, but I thank you all for the company an' for the play."

Longarm stood and touched the brim of his Stetson to the gents at the table. He yawned again and stretched, then ambled out into the street and down the block to Hart's Café. He had eaten there before and liked it. It was cheaper than the restaurant at the Fairplay Hotel and just as good if not as fancy.

He took a table in the back corner where he could have his back to the wall, set his hat on the seat of the vacant chair to his right, and gave the approaching waiter a smile and a nod.

"No need for that menu in your hand, friend. I know what I want. A beef steak, or elk if you got it, either one thick an' juicy an' fried in tallow. A heap o' fried taters to go with that steak. An' coffee. Lots o' coffee hot an' black. Oh, yeah. Biscuits with plenty o' gravy."

The waiter grinned. "You're a cowhand, aren't you?"

Longarm smiled and said, "Now, how could you know a thing like that?"

He already knew the answer and was betting that this waiter did too.

"That's a trail drover's meal, of course. What outfit are you working for?"

Longarm shook his head. "That's been a long time ago, but the taste for good, solid food remains. You?"

The fellow shrugged. "You see what I'm doing these days. I gave up a good job. Wintered over in Denver a couple years back and got the gold fever. Up here I discovered that these mountains aren't chock full of gold lying around waiting for me to find it. Well, I've learned my lesson. Come next spring I'll be down in south Texas looking to hook on with a trail crew. You?"

"Me, I took steady work down in Denver too. I'm still at it," Longarm said.

"Well, good luck to you," the waiter said before he went back to the kitchen to turn in Longarm's order. He was back quickly with coffee and a piece of pie. "On the house," he said, "from one out-of-place ranny to another."

Longarm saluted the gent with a finger to the forehead and reminded himself to give the man a generous tip when all was said and done.

He was about to speak when there was a disturbance two tables over. A nicely dressed gentleman was bending over a flustered young woman with chestnut hair and a throat-high blouse, white shirtwaist, and long, dark skirt. She was fairly attractive but no raving beauty.

"I won't take no for an answer," the man was saying, his voice becoming louder as he became more and more agitated.

"That is the only answer you shall receive, James."

"Now look here, Louise . . ."

"No, James, *you* look here. I am not interested in you. I am not interested in any boyfriend, not you or anyone else. Why oh why can you not understand something as simple as that?"

"Do you think you're better than me, Louise? Too good for me? Well, I'll show you. I will . . ."

Before the man could finish his sentence, the waiter had him by the arm, yanking him away from the lady at the table.

James responded with a swift, underhand punch to the waiter's belly and a knee in the man's groin. The waiter turned pale and dropped to the floor, doubled over and holding his balls.

James tried to return his attention to the young woman, but this time it was Longarm who hauled him away from her table.

"You're causin' a fuss," Longarm growled between clenched teeth. "Leave her be or you could get yourself hurt."

"Not by you, mister." James threw a punch intended to land in Longarm's soft belly and double him over the way a similar blow had their waiter.

Except Longarm did not *have* a soft belly, and he had seen the blow coming in time to tighten his muscles and prepare for it.

James's fist might as well have been punching the bole of an aspen tree.

James looked up, gaping.

Longarm smiled. And dropped him with a hard right cross.

The man went down like a felled tree and stayed there.

Longarm turned to the waiter and helped him to his feet. "Sorry 'bout this," he said. Then he turned his attention to the lady James had been bothering. "Is there anything my new friend and me can do for you, miss?"

She looked down at James, who was still on the floor but beginning to stir. "Yes, I . . . If you don't mind, if it would not be too much of a bother, could you dine with me, please? I'm worried about what he might do if I am alone this evening."

"Of course, miss. Have you finished your meal? No? Then please. Move over to my table with me. Would that be all right?"

"Yes, I would like that."

Longarm bowed to her, glanced at James, who was crawling onto his feet, and took the lady by the elbow, guiding her to one of the vacant chairs at his table.

Over the lady's shoulder he winked at their waiter, who looked like he would enjoy another crack at James, but this time when he was expecting the blow.

Chapter 22

"Would you please do me another favor, sir?" the lady asked. She had, Longarm noticed, very large and expressive brown eyes. Pretty eyes.

"Of course, miss. Pretty much anything you ask," he said.

"Would you please walk me home? It isn't far, and I am afraid James might accost me along the way. He knows where I live, and he is a violent man."

"I'd be honored," Longarm assured her.

They finished their meal, and Longarm left one of his recently won quarter eagles to pay for what could not possibly have been more than a dollar's worth of food.

He retrieved his Stetson from the seat of the adjacent chair and helped Louise with her chair, then placed her shawl around her shoulders.

"Thank you, sir."

Longarm followed the lady outside. He did not say anything, but he was fairly sure he spotted James lurking in the mouth of an alley across the street from Hart's. The man stayed where he was and did not approach Longarm and Louise.

"It isn't far," she said.

"Won't matter," he told her. "I'll be right here beside you."

Louise lived only a block and a half behind the Fairplay Hotel. When they reached her door, Longarm removed his hat and half bowed. "Ma'am."

"May I ask you one more thing?"

"Anything," he assured her.

"Would you come inside with me? I don't want to be alone just now."

"That would be my pleasure," he said.

He stopped at the doorway while Louise went ahead of him—she knew where the furniture was placed, after all—and lighted a lamp.

"There," she said brightly. "Now you can come in. Sit down, Custis. Here if you like."

He took the much used reading chair beside the lamp and put his feet up on the stool positioned in front of it. The chair was obviously Louise's own favorite spot. A book with a page marker stuck midway through it lay on the small table beside the chair.

Louise had mentioned during dinner that she taught school here. She certainly dressed the part of a prim and proper lady schoolteacher. When she offered a drink, he was assuming that she would have tea . . . not his favorite beverage, although he could gag it down when he had to.

"Yes, ma'am," he said.

"Please don't tell anyone about this," she said as she knelt beside a small, ornate cabinet.

His eyebrows went up.

"The school board," she added, "require all teachers to take an oath of abstinence." She laughed. "I would be a great disappointment to them if they knew."

Exactly what she did not want the school board to know became clear when she pulled out a bottle of Four Roses blended whiskey.

"Just a moment," she said. "I'll get some glasses."

She disappeared into another room and seemed to be

taking quite a while just to pick up a couple glasses. The reason for that was apparent when she returned.

Louise had let her hair down, both literally and figuratively. Her chestnut hair shimmered in the lamplight. And now the high-neck blouse and shirtwaist had been replaced by a crimson silk robe with Chinese characters on the front and a fire-breathing dragon sewn in gold thread on the back.

"I hope you don't mind if I make myself comfortable," she said.

"Not at all."

It seemed that prim and proper Louise had a very nice figure that she had been hiding under her workday clothing.

She poured two fingers of whiskey into each of two glasses and handed one to him. "To your good health," she said, tossing the liquor back as deftly as any man could have.

Longarm took a swallow of his but put the glass aside when Louise slid comfortably into his lap, wrapping her arms around his neck and smiling. "Do you mind?"

His answer was the logical one. He kissed her, his free hand slipping inside the front of her robe to find and cup a firm, hard-tipped breast.

Chapter 23

"In there," Louise whispered into the ear she had been nibbling on while he carried her.

Longarm aimed the two of them in the direction indicated. A little light seeped in from the lamp in the living room, enough for him to easily see the double bed—he appreciated the lady's foresight in her choice of bed—in the middle of the room. He placed Louise gently down with her head on a pillow.

He sat on the edge of the bed beside her and plucked at the knot that was loosely holding her robe together.

The knot came away easily, and the silky material fell open to reveal pale, pink-tipped breasts, a flat belly and a thick muff of brown curls.

Louise was smiling as she watched his expression. "Do you like?" she whispered.

"I like," he assured her.

"Show me," she challenged.

Her tongue was hot and her breath was sweet. He lay beside her kissing and fondling her for some time, then Louise squirmed out from under him. She knelt between his knees and toyed with his balls for a moment before she bent down and peeled his foreskin back.

She took him into her mouth. Only the tip at first. Then the head. Finally the shaft, drawing him deeper and deeper inside her mouth, until he was almost fully engulfed in the heat of her.

With a final hard shove she pushed him past the tight constriction at the back of her throat, past the ring of cartilage there so that his entire length filled her. Her lips pressed against the base of his cock and her nose pushed hard into the hair at the bottom of his belly.

"Nice," he mumbled when she started to bob up and down on his dick, the feeling seeming to intensify with every stroke into her mouth and every withdrawal.

She made the sensation even better by sucking hard on him each time she pulled away, taking his foreskin up and down with her movement.

"Really nice," he said, louder this time.

He reached down and grabbed a handful of brown hair, hanging on like a bronc peeler trying to stay with a rank pony. Louise shook her head and laughed.

She pulled away from him long enough to claim, "I like it rough. Do me rough, baby. Use me hard."

Louise tried to go back to his prick, but Longarm yanked her hair. Hard. And jerked her away from him. She lost her balance and sprawled onto her back at his side.

Longarm squeezed her tits. Hard. She yelped and opened herself to him. "Yes, please. Hurt me."

It was not Custis Long's custom to hurt a woman. But . . .

He hauled her up beside him, shifted over between her legs, and plunged down onto her. Into her. Hard. Fast. Pounding her belly with his own, the sound of it like one slap after another.

Louise cried out when he filled her pussy. She clutched him with her arms and with her legs as well, and she none too gently bit his shoulder when she shuddered throughout her body in an earth-shaking climax.

Longarm continued to pump until he too came.

He drifted off to sleep, still inside her, still on top of her. Louise woke him some time later.

"Reach under the bed," she whispered. "There's a paddle. Spank me. Please, darling. Paddle my ass. Punish me for being such a wicked woman."

The paddle was where she claimed, and it was late by the time he got back to sleep.

Come morning, Louise giggled and said, "Now you know why us schoolteachers wear high-neck clothes and long sleeves, darling. And I swear, I'll be feeling this all day long. Every time my skirt brushes against my skin and every time I sit down on that hard chair behind my desk. I really should buy a soft pillow for such occasions as this." She laughed and said, "I'll bet my ass is red as a beet."

"Yep. 'Tis," he told her. "But it's a pretty shade o' red. And for that matter a mighty pretty ass."

Louise laughed. "Will you still be in town tonight?"

"No," he said, "but I'll be wishin' that I was." He kissed her and said, "Now get your pretty ass outa this bed an' make me some coffee."

"Yes. Oh, yes. Anything you say, Custis." She was smiling when she jumped to do his bidding.

Longarm figured he had had a much more enjoyable night than Eddie Curen, Jr., over in that jail cell.

Chapter 24

It was nearly dawn when Longarm slipped out of Louise's little house and headed back toward his hotel. He needed to wash and shave and get his things together before that stagecoach rolled at seven-fifteen.

He stood for a moment in the cool of the predawn air and reached for a cheroot.

Longarm's hand stopped short of the cigar, however. There was something . . . something moving in the deeper shadows across the street, and he did not want to ruin his night vision by striking a match. Not just then.

Slowly, as if intending to lean against one of the roof columns, Longarm shifted to the side. His right hand slid his .45 from the leather.

Suddenly breaking from the shadows, he dashed across the street two houses down from where he thought he had seen that movement. When he was halfway across, a spear of bright flame licked toward him, followed almost immediately by the sharp crack of a small-caliber pistol.

"Dammit, James, leave her be," Longarm barked.

"She's my woman," James shouted, still in the shadows. "You messed with her."

"She ain't your woman," Longarm returned, reaching

the side of the house on the same side of the street as the would-be assassin. "Now, quit this before you get hurt. You ain't no good at shooting people, but I am, so's you'd better quit while you're still alive."

"I'm going to kill you, mister," James shouted.

"Hush up, James. You're waking the whole neighborhood."

Longarm held his fire. He really did not want to shoot the man. But he would if he had to. "Let's talk about this, James. Come along with me. We'll go over to Hart's and have some breakfast."

"You go to hell, mister."

"Oh, I more than likely will. But not today and not by your hand. Now come outa there and calm down."

Longarm thought he could hear sobbing coming from those shadows. Like a grown man crying. That made him feel worse than being shot at had. Grown men don't cry, dammit.

"C'mon, James. Talk to me. There's no need for you to be all het up here."

"There's no-no-nothing to talk about."

"Sure there is," Longarm called, moving silently across the front of the house where he was sheltering, moving closer to James, holding the .45 but hoping he could avoid using it. "We'll have us some breakfast. Maybe some deep-dish apple pie. They got good pie at Hart's. Fried taters and a beefsteak. How's steak for breakfast sound to you?"

James did not answer. Longarm heard movement over there. He pondered whether he could rush the stupid son of a bitch and wrestle the pistol away from him before he could do any real damage with it.

All up and down the block lights were beginning to glow yellow behind drawn shades as the shooting and the shouting roused people out of their beds.

"You and me, James. We can invite Louise too. She might come along with us. I can't promise that, of course. It ain't up to me, but we can walk over there and make the invite. What do you say, James?" He paused. "James? What're you doing there? I can hear you moving. Where you going now?"

There was silence for what seemed like a long moment.

Then a muffled gunshot broke the silence.

The gunshot and then the sound of a body falling.

"Oh, shit, James, you stupid son of a bitch," Longarm groaned.

He shoved his Colt back into the leather and went to see what the dumb bastard had gone and done.

Chapter 25

A slender young man—downright skinny, actually—showed up wearing a badge and carrying a worried look.

"What's going on? Someone said they heard gunshots."

Longarm stepped out of the crowd that had gathered, some of them wearing nightshirts stuffed into their trousers, in the aftermath of the excitement.

"I'm a deputy U.S. marshal," Longarm announced, sticking his hand out to meet the Fairplay town marshal. "This fellow took a couple shots at me. Then the dumb bastard shot himself." Longarm shook his head. "Shot himself in the belly, can you believe it? Idiot could linger for days with a wound like that."

"Gut-shot, you say?" the town marshal said, kneeling beside James and trying with no success to pull James's hands away from his belly. A nickel-plated breaktop .32 lay in the dirt beside him. The marshal picked the revolver up and stuck it into his pocket.

"Who are you, by the way?" Longarm asked, kneeling beside the marshal.

"Ben Caulfield," the marshal said.

Longarm offered his hand again. This time the local lawman took it. "Custis Long," Longarm said as they shook.

"Oh, yes. I've heard of you." He grinned. "Some of what I heard was good."

"That puts me ahead o' my usual pace then."

Caulfield motioned toward James. "Do you know what this is about?"

Longarm nodded. "He kept saying something about the lady across the street, schoolteacher I think he said, kept saying something about her being his woman. Or anyway him wanting her to belong to him. I don't know that she feels the same way about it. The way he was acting I got the idea she didn't favor him and that's why he was so . . . what's the word I want here . . . despondent."

"So he shot himself?" Caulfield said.

Longarm nodded. "In the belly. I mean, how stupid can a man be. If he wants to kill himself, fine. But shoot himself in the head, not the gut. And with a bigger pistol than that pipsqueak thing you got in your pocket. He should at least get himself a man-size gun to do the job."

Caulfield grunted and stood up. Longarm stood as well, reaching into his coat for a cheroot. Caulfield snapped a match aflame and held it to the tip of the slender cigar for him.

"Can I offer you one?" Longarm asked.

The town marshal shook his head and grinned again. "Thanks, but I don't smoke."

"If you tell me you don't drink either, I'll start examining you for a halo."

"Let's not get carried away with this clean living bullshit," Caulfield said. "I can only lay off one vice at a time. Speaking of drinking, would you like to walk over to Ike's with me for a drink or two while you fill out my paperwork?"

"Who's Ike and what paperwork?" Longarm asked.

"Ike's is the saloon around that corner there, and the paperwork is the report I'll be needing you to fill out before you leave town."

"Listen, Marshal, I got a prisoner up on the third floor

over there, and I got to get him down to Denver for arraignment. I'm probably already late for the stagecoach down to the railroad."

"You're right about that. The coach pulled out of here about ten minutes ago. Which means you have plenty of time to spend on that paperwork for me. With or without the drink—your choice."

"With," Longarm said. He had not yet had breakfast, but there was no reason why breakfast couldn't be boiled eggs and pickled sausages off a free lunch platter. And a drink or two to go with them. He sighed. "All right, Marshal. Lead the way. We'll get your reports made. But shouldn't you have someone haul this poor son of a bitch off to see a doc, so he can at least slug down some laudanum and ease the pain while he goes about the business of dying."

"Oh, right. Thanks for reminding me." Caulfield quickly gathered some volunteers and instructed them where to take James. "Tell Doc Harris that I'll be along directly to get his statement if he's able to give one and to complete the reports about him."

"Now, where is this Ike's place?" Longarm asked once James had been carried off to Doc Harris's. At this point he was more than ready for a shot of rye for breakfast.

Chapter 26

The rye was good and the beer chaser nice and crisp. Better yet, Ike's Mexican . . . wife, woman, squeeze, whatever the hell she was . . . had a fine touch with chorizo, eggs, and tortillas. He felt a damn sight better once he surrounded all of those for his breakfast.

"Are you satisfied with your reports?" he asked Caulfield, who had sat by drinking black coffee and asking questions while he made sure everything was set down in writing.

Caulfield nodded. "I'll go get Wilcox's statement now if he's in any condition to give one."

"Mind if I tag along? I'm curious what the man will say," Longarm said.

"You're welcome to come with me, but mind you, I'll ask the questions," Caulfield said.

"Oh, that suits me just fine. They're your reports, after all. I'm just a witness to this one."

"You never fired a shot? You're sure?" Caulfield asked for probably the twentieth time since they sat down at the table in Ike's saloon.

Longarm sighed and dragged his Colt out of the leather. He flipped the loading gate open and dropped the cartridges out into his palm, then handed the revolver to the town lawman.

"You been with me this whole time, so you know I haven't had a chance to clean this piece. Take a sniff at the muzzle. You'll see it ain't been fired recent."

"Oh, I believe you," Caulfield said. But he took the empty .45 from Longarm and smelled both the muzzle and the cylinder before handing it back. "Like I said. I believe you." He stood up from the table. "Come along then. We'll walk over to see Doc."

The doctor's home, with an office set up in what should have been the dining room, was only a few blocks away. But then in Fairplay almost everything was within a few blocks. The town was not very big.

A shingle hanging out front read: GEO. M. HARRIS, M.D.

Harris turned out to be half the age Longarm would have expected. He assumed that a genuine physician stuck away in a small town in the mountains would have to be an older gent looking for retirement or something close to it. Harris in fact turned out to be a young and energetic fireball of a man.

He was almost as skinny as Ben Caulfield, and despite his young age he was losing his hair. What he had remaining was dark blond and in need of cutting.

Caulfield performed the introductions.

"Your man is in here," Harris said, leading the way to a back bedroom that was barely large enough to accommodate a canvas cot and a tiny bedside table with a large lamp on it.

James Wilcox had been stripped to the waist. A square of folded cloth had been laid over the middle of his belly, obviously where the bullet had gone in.

"Bullet still in there?" Longarm asked.

Harris nodded. "A small-caliber like this one must have been wouldn't be strong enough to come out the back. It's still in there, and I won't risk taking away what little time he has left by probing for the slug. After all, that would serve no purpose. He won't survive the wound."

"You're sure about that, George?" Caulfield asked.

Again the doctor nodded. "When I lean down close to the wound, I can clearly smell stomach acids and feces."

"Feces?" the town marshal asked. "What the hell is feces?"

"Shit to the likes of you, you dumb bastard," the doctor retorted, giving Longarm a clear enough indication that these two men were friends and probably very good friends at that.

"Can we talk to him?" Caulfield asked.

"You can talk until you're blue in the face, Ben. I doubt he will answer. Right now he is pretty much wrapped up in his own miseries."

"May I?" Longarm asked.

The doctor shrugged and stepped aside.

Longarm knelt beside the dying man and said, "You remember me, James. You tried to shoot me out in the street this morning. Are you willin' to talk a little now?"

Wilcox at least rolled his head to the side and opened his eyes so he could see Longarm there beside him. "You bastard," he said.

"Yeah, that's me. You want to tell the marshal here why you done what you done?"

"Should . . . should've been you." Wilcox shifted his gaze from Longarm to Ben Caulfield. "It's Louise. Bitch is too . . . Ah, geez that hurts . . . Bitch thinks she's too good for me, but she fucked him, all right."

Caulfield looked at Longarm and raised an eyebrow.

"The lady was afraid of this man," Longarm said. "You can ask the waiter at Hart's. He was giving her trouble there last night. I walked her home and stayed in the parlor drinking coffee and kind of standing guard over her. When I came outside to head back to my hotel room this morning, he shot at me. Twice. I have no idea where those shots went. Nowhere close to me, I'm sure of that. I ducked out of the way. Had my revolver in hand but never needed to fire it. Then he blew a hole in his own stomach. Which is where you came in. You already know everything as happened after that."

Caulfield nodded. "Is that about right, James?"

"Except he didn't just stand guard. He fucked the school-teacher sure as I'm laying here," Wilcox said, obviously distraught at the thought.

"He says he stood guard," Caulfield said, "so my report will say that he stood guard against you, James. That's the way it is."

"Bastard. I shoulda known you'd take his side." Wilcox rolled his head to the other side so he could not see the two lawmen. He did not say another word after that.

"You might as well leave now, gentlemen," Doc Harris said. "I'm about to give him another heavy dose of laudanum, so I doubt he would be able to answer any questions even if he wanted to."

Wilcox was obviously in the throes of agony, but he came to his senses enough to gulp down the draft of bitter laudanum. Shortly after he took the medication, his eyes rolled back in his head and he found the relief of a drugged slumber.

Caulfield turned to leave. Longarm followed close behind him.

"I'll come back this afternoon," the town lawman said. "He may be able to tell me more then."

"Get him pissed off enough an' he'll tell you plenty," Longarm suggested.

"Some of which may be true." Caulfield shrugged. "Or not."

"You got your reports. Can I buy you a drink?" Longarm offered.

Caulfield grinned. "Maybe just one."

The two men returned to Ike's saloon. They were still there propping up the bar at noon.

Chapter 27

"I thought you said I'd only be here overnight," the prisoner complained the following morning when the on-duty deputy—Longarm did not know him—unlocked the cell to let the man out.

"I did, but like the saying goes, shit happens. Now, put your hands behind your back. I want to put cuffs on you," Longarm said.

"Can I tell you something, Marshal?" Curen asked.

"I suppose so."

The prisoner smiled. "Marshal, you look like shit your own self."

Longarm grunted. "Two nights without sleep will do that to you."

"Oh." Curen thought for a moment, then grinned and said, "Lucky streak?"

"You could say so." Longarm's eyes were gritty with fatigue after two nights with the energetic—and very imaginative—schoolteacher. He did not regret the time spent with her, but now he wanted to get on his way back to Denver and a job that would surely be more interesting than this one. Almost any other job would be an improvement over playing nursemaid to a dull-witted, easygoing prisoner like this one.

He yawned and stepped out of the way so Curen could pass in the narrow aisle outside the bars.

"How are we going from here?" Curen asked.

"Stagecoach down to Frisco, railroad after that. We should get to Denver sometime tonight. You'll be put up tonight in the federal holding cells, then in the morning you'll be taken over to the courthouse for arraignment."

"And after that?"

Longarm shrugged. "After that, it'll be up to whatever judge you draw. Some go easier than others. For theft from the mails, you're looking at, oh, five to seven years, I'd think, so bail might be set kinda high. Won't matter. Your papa is surely good for it."

"What about my lawyer? Will he be there?"

Longarm shrugged again. "You'd have to ask him that. He's certainly allowed to be. Normally would be, I'd think, but I can't tell you that for certain sure."

Curen sighed. "This is all so different from what I woulda thought. Say, could I ask you something else?"

"You can ask. Might or might not get the answer you want."

"Could you put these handcuffs in front of my belly, please. It feels awful awkward in the back like this. I'll promise not to give you no trouble."

Longarm pondered that for a moment, then nodded. The man had been no trouble so far. There was no indication he intended to change that now.

Longarm got his handcuff key out, unlocked one bracelet, and brought the man's hands around to the front, then snapped the other cuff on again.

"That's much better. Thank you."

"You're welcome. Ready to go now?"

"Yes, sir, wherever you say."

Longarm motioned Curen ahead of him through the narrow corridor and down the steep flights of stairs to the ground floor.

Chapter 28

The train reached Denver about half past eight. Longarm waited with his prisoner until the passenger car emptied, then took him down onto the platform.

"Watch your step, Eddie." He took Curen by the elbow to steady him on the step down to solid footing, then led him over to one of the hansom cabs waiting beyond the platform.

Curen was still handcuffed in front of his body, so he had no trouble climbing into the cab on his own.

"County jail, please," Longarm called up to the driver, then got into the cab behind his prisoner.

The hansom lurched into motion, swaying and clomping its way through the familiar streets until they reached the Denver County jail where federal prisoners were accommodated while awaiting trial.

Longarm paid the cab fare, then took Curen inside. He got the prisoner signed in pending arraignment, then gratefully took another cab home to his rooming house.

A note was fastened to the door to his room. Written in Henry's meticulous hand, it read: "Boss wants you present at Curen's arraignment just in case lawyer demands testimony by arresting officer. Report here afterward."

That, however, was something for tomorrow. Longarm

went in, stripped, and gratefully collapsed onto his own familiar bed.

Come morning, a wash and a shave left him feeling mostly human. He dressed, had a quick bite of breakfast, and went outside to find a cab. He rode over to the Denver County jail and went in to find that Edward Curen, Jr., had already been transported over to the courthouse with other prisoners whose arraignments were set for that morning.

Billy Vail's clerk—and right hand, if the truth be known—Henry was already present in the courtroom, seated beside a gentleman in a somewhat faded suit coat and batwing shirt. Both Henry and this newcomer rose when Longarm approached.

"Long, I'd like you to meet Donald Ware. Mr. Ware was postmaster in Curen Town until recently."

Longarm shook hands with the man but raised an eyebrow. "Used to be postmaster, you say?"

"Mr. Curen Senior has, um, influence," Ware said. "He had me removed from my posting. Which is just as well. I didn't much care for it up there anyway. The postmaster general assures me he can find another position for me soon."

"I wish you luck, Mr. Ware," Longarm said. "You sure did the right thing about pressing the charge. We can't be putting up with theft from the mail, no matter the reason."

"I agree completely, Mr. Long," Ware said. "You say Eddie Junior will be here this morning?"

"Yes, of course. I brought him in last night. There he sits, Mr. Ware. In the jail box there."

"I don't see Eddie there, Mr. Long," Ware said.

"Right there, sir. Betwixt the big fellow with the bandage on his head and the man in the red-and-black checked shirt."

Ware looked closely for a moment, then turned to Longarm and said, "But you are mistaken, Mr. Long. That isn't Eddie Curen, it is Harold Bayne, one of the town layabouts."

"Come again? That ain't Eddie?"

"Oh, no," Ware said, shaking his head. "Everybody up there knows Harold. He is a little soft in the head. Not badly so, you understand. He does odd jobs around town."

"Well . . . shit!" Longarm said, the words coming out almost as a snarl. He spun around and rushed away from the courthouse without bothering to go to the marshal's office or to file a report.

"Harold Bayne!" he grumbled aloud.

Chapter 29

It was the middle of the night before Longarm reached Fair-play again. Along the way he'd remembered that he had left Harold Bayne still in the custody of the jailers in the Denver County lockup. Remembered it but did not feel compelled to do anything about it immediately. The son of a bitch could just sit there until Longarm returned. Anyway he was probably being well paid to imitate Edward Curen, Jr. Bastards. Both of them.

"Do you still have those horses from down in Manitou?" Longarm asked the hostler at the Fairplay livery stable and feedlot after shaking the man out of his bed.

"No, sir. I sent them back down, just the way you asked me to. Tied them on behind a stagecoach headed that way. They should be there by now."

"Well, shit," Longarm grumbled. It was an expression he was using more and more since finding out that the man he'd thought was Eddie Curen, Jr., was in fact Harold Bayne. "How about another pair of saddle horses. Decent ones. They don't have to be great."

"Marshal, the only thing I have in the barn that would take a saddle at all is that big brown mule there, and there's only the one of him."

"Shit," Longarm barked again. He was becoming frustrated to the point of distraction now. "I got to have two."

The hostler shrugged. "I could send down to Manitou for them horses you brought up here. They could be back here in a couple days, I'd think."

"I'm not going to sit around here for the next two days waiting for transportation. What do you have that will get me over to Curen Town and then me and one other person back here again?"

The hostler thought for a moment, then said, "I have that nice doctor buggy over there and that same big mule. He'll go between poles as good as under saddle or do pretty much anything else you need him to. Would that do you?"

"Mister, if it will get me there an' back again, I'll ride a buffalo calf pulling a snow sled. I'll take it."

"Same deal as before? Government voucher?"

Longarm nodded. "That's right, neighbor. Now introduce me to this big-ass mule of yours an' let me get on the road. I want to make Curen Town with plenty o' daylight remaining."

He had about decided that he was not going to get any sleep until this miserable job was finished, and anyway he was too thoroughly pissed off to sleep now.

"Show me how this harness goes, will ya?"

Chapter 30

The mule acted like it had never learned how to become tired. Longarm pushed its gait and drove into the outskirts of Curen Town before noon.

He did not stop at the livery but rolled on past and drew to a halt outside Ed Curen's headquarters. He tethered the mule to a porch support pole and stalked inside without knocking.

As before, the big man was seated behind his desk. A gent who looked like he might be a bookkeeper was seated in a chair in front of Curen's desk.

"Well," Curen declared when he saw Longarm, "Marshal. I am, um, surprised to see you here. I thought . . ."

"You thought you could pull the wool over my eyes," Longarm snapped. "Well, you done that. But you couldn't keep it there. Harold Bayne was recognized. That let's the cat outa the bag, don't it. Now, you son of a bitch . . . you!" he barked at the visitor. "Stay right where you are lest I get ideas that'd be bad for your health. An' you," he turned his attention back to Curen, "you fucked up royally. You want to be appointed United States marshal and start climbing the political ladder?"

Longarm took a deep breath and bulled his way on. "Ain't

gonna happen," he snapped. "The attorney general sure as hell ain't gonna give an appointment to a man with an obstuction of justice conviction on his record."

"But . . ."

"Don't try an' interrupt me, dammit. You set there an' shut your mouth an' listen for a change. I don't really give a shit about your son. That'll all be up to a judge. But you, you, I am gonna set in that courtroom every minute o' your trial. I'm gonna testify against you, Curen. The jailer an' half the courtroom full o' folks down in Denver are gonna testify against you tryin' to pass off some poor son of a bitch as your son. An' I personally will see to it that you spend some time in the hoosgow. What's more, I am personally gonna make sure that the attorney general knows all about this little play o' yours. That is gonna fuck you up, mister. I can guarantee it. Now, if you don't want to make it worse, I strongly suggest you trot that missing son o' yours out an' watch while I put handcuffs on him."

Longarm was steaming. It was a wonder wisps of it did not escape from his ears.

He stood over Curen, fists planted on his hips lest he plant them into Ed Curen's face, a face which suddenly was drained of all color.

"You . . . you can't . . . can't . . ."

"Bullshit, I can't. Watch me an' see. Now, I am gonna walk over to the café and get me a meal. Then I am gonna come back out and climb into the buggy I got parked outside. I expect to see Eddie Curen, Jr., setting there meek an' polite an' waiting for me to take him down to Denver for that arraignment, just like he was supposed to to begin with. Do you understand me, you sorry piece o' dog shit? *Well, do you?*" Longarm's voice kept rising until those last few words were shouted.

Without waiting for an answer, he spun on his heels and marched the hell out of Ed Curen's office.

He was mad. He was also halfway to starvation, or so the rumbling in his belly suggested.

"Cock-suckin' son of a bitch," he mumbled on his way out, not specifying exactly who he meant by that. "Shit-eatin' bastard."

A matronly woman passing by on the sidewalk overheard and started to say something to him, but when she got a look at the expression on Longarm's face she merely gathered up her skirts and hurried away down the block without speaking.

Chapter 31

Longarm had no idea if his dinner was good or not. He gobbled it down but was so angry that he was not aware of tasting it. He kept eating until it was a wonder his belly did not burst.

"Another piece of pie?" the waiter asked eventually.

Longarm shook his head. "No, sir, four is enough for me."

"You know I have to charge you extra for all that pie."

"The sign out front says pie comes with the meal."

"Right. The first piece did. The other three you have to pay for."

"All right, then, dammit. It ain't worth fighting over." Longarm dug into his trousers and came up with a fifty-cent piece. "That cover it?"

"Yes, sir. That covers it just fine."

Longarm grunted and surrendered his half dollar. He stood, stretched, and reached for his hat before dropping another dime down for a tip.

"Thank you, sir."

"If I want you to pack me a lunch, can you do that?" Longarm asked.

"Like for a picnic or something? Sure, we can do that. Just tell me what you want and when you want it ready. I'll charge you for the meal and there will be a deposit on the basket, but I'll make sure it's fixed up real nice."

Obviously, Longarm thought, the fellow assumed he would be squiring some young lady for his picnic. There seemed no point in telling him that his "date" would be Eddie Curen, Jr. Nor that the basket would end up down in Denver, for Longarm had no desire to return to Curen Town once he got shut of it this time.

He nodded to the waiter and settled his Stetson onto his head, then stepped out onto the board sidewalk.

And jumped right back in again when a bullet thudded into the doorjamb, sending a spray of pine splinters into his face.

Chapter 32

Longarm palmed his .45, dropped down to a knee, and carefully peered out.

He saw a puff of white smoke coming from the doorway of a grocery across the street.

Longarm let out his best imitation of a Rebel yell and, revolver in hand and still screaming, charged directly at the smoke.

He burst through the doorway and ran smack into a man wearing a grocer's once-white apron, bowling the man over.

Longarm wound up standing over the terrified grocer, pointing the .45 into the man's face.

The grocer, he saw with disgust, was smoking a cigarette.

"You got a gun on you?" he demanded.

"N-n-no, I . . . I don't own one."

"You didn't shoot at me just now?"

"I haven't shot a gun in twenty years."

"Then who the hell did?" Longarm was beginning to go from fury to embarrassment. The change left him feeling shaky.

"I don't know, sir." The man on the floor looked like he had gone well past shaky. The poor son of a bitch looked like he was about to piss his pants. Or already had. It would have been impossible to see behind the white duck apron.

"Well, shit," Longarm grumbled. He stuffed his Colt back into the leather and reached down to offer the grocer a hand up. "I'm sorry. Somebody shot at me just now an' I seen the smoke from your quirly come out the door there."

The grocer took Longarm's hand and accepted the help getting upright once again. He brushed himself off and shuddered. "You startled me," the man said.

"Who was it shot at me, mister?" Longarm asked, calmly this time.

The grocer shook his head. "Sorry. I didn't see. I heard the shot but didn't see who fired it. Say, are you that fellow, uh, Long? Custis Long?"

"That's me, why?"

The man gave him a speculative look, then shook his head again. "It just isn't in me, I guess."

"What isn't?"

"Murder," the grocer said with a sigh. "I'm just not the sort to kill a man, I suppose. Not even for five thousand."

"Five thousand?" Longarm asked.

"You don't know?"

"Obviously not. What're you talking about?"

"Word has been going around the street for the past hour or so that the man who kills you can collect five thousand dollars, no questions asked and no charges filed." He sighed again. "Five thousand. Jesus, that's ten years' wages. Anybody could use that much money. All at one time? It's a fortune."

"Yeah, ain't that the simple stinkin' truth," Longarm muttered as he turned away and looked out into the street.

Every doorway or alley mouth out there, every window or trash heap, could hide someone who wanted to collect that bounty on Custis Long's head.

That would be the way Edward Curen intended to keep alive his hopes for a career in high political circles. Get rid of Longarm, and the threat of arrest and conviction would be removed, at least that was the way he must be thinking about it, never mind the fact that Longarm was a deputy United States marshal. If he were to disappear up here in the mountains, other deputies would follow. Longarm's brother officers would come and they would find out about the murder—his murder—and they would follow that trail right to the doorstep of Ed Curen, Sr. It would be too late to help Longarm, but it would not do Curen a whole hell of a lot of good either. One would be shot down; the other would hang.

And Eddie Curen, Jr., would go to jail for theft from the mails regardless.

Longarm took a deep breath and slowly exhaled. The dumb son of a bitch, he mused. With the help of a good lawyer, Eddie Junior likely could have gotten off with probation and a harsh talking to. Now both father and son would be behind bars. And that was at the very least. The father might still hang if Longarm's luck were to run out in this miserable little dog turd of a town.

He checked his .45 again to reassure himself that it was loose in the holster and readily available.

Then he stepped out onto the sidewalk.

Chapter 33

He turned toward the doctor buggy that was parked in the next block, thinking this might be a good time to go ask Billy to send some backup deputies, and only then realized that while the buggy was still there, the mule was not. The poles were on the ground, no animal between them, even though the buggy itself was where he had left it.

Come to think of it, he realized, there were no horses tied to the posts and hitch rails up and down the street.

He was fairly sure there had been half a dozen or more visible when he went into the café for dinner. Now . . . nothing. The street was empty except for ruts and the occasional pile of horse shit.

Obviously Ed Senior did not want him leaving town. Except for burial, that is.

What Curen did not seem to realize was that Longarm was in no mood for dying right now. Someday, sure. But not now, dammit. He still had things to do, among them being to take both father and son in to face Lady Justice.

He stepped into the mouth of an alley that was two buildings short of Ed Curen's offices and wondered just how widespread the knowledge of that bounty offer might be. Had everyone in the whole damn town been told about it?

And if so, how many of them would have the nerve to make a try toward collecting it?

There would be some like that grocer back there who wanted to make money but not the deed.

There were undoubtedly a good many others who would be willing to make an attempt to collect it.

Longarm's scalp tingled. Nerves, he decided, and that was something he was not accustomed to.

It felt strange, knowing that anyone in this whole damned town, man or woman, boy or beast, might want to gun him down.

He palmed his Colt again and bolted for the buggy. There might be no mule there to pull it, but his carpetbag was there, and in that was the telegraph key that he always carried.

With the key in hand, he could slip out of town, climb a suitable telegraph pole—that is, one that was fairly well hidden from any ambush sites—and wire Billy about the situation up here.

He had not gotten three strides out of the alley before a pair of shots boomed out, one coming from either side of the street.

One lead slug struck the wooden siding of the building on his left, while the other thudded into the hardened mud of a rut in the street behind him, sending a spray of clods into the air.

The bastards had him in a cross fire. Not the very best place to be.

The buggy, it seemed, was out of bounds, at least for now. Perhaps he could reach it after dark, but nightfall was hours away and he could well be dead long short of that.

He stopped and, having no target to shoot at, did not even bother to send a return bullet.

Besides, his spare ammunition was in that carpetbag in the buggy. All he had on him was what was in the .45 and the handful of cartridges that he customarily carried in his coat pocket.

He just plain was not equipped to engage in a prolonged gunfight.

Longarm bolted back for the relative safety of the alley. He pressed himself up against the wall at his back and took a few deep breaths.

Now he knew what an elk felt like when there were hunters stalking it in the woods.

He looked into the street as best he could but saw no human movement, not the hunters or anyone else. Curen Town might as well have been a ghost town for all the activity he could see.

Longarm took another few deep breaths, then withdrew from the alley mouth and crept slowly toward the back of the alley.

What he needed to do, he decided, was to get down to that livery stable, where he could steal a horse and head for Fairplay.

He was not running away, he assured himself. This was what was termed a strategic withdrawal, the operative word there being "withdrawal." And he intended to withdraw the shit out of this situation.

Chapter 34

A sound! Behind him. It was too faint for him to consciously identify and could have been something as innocent as a bird dropping down to the earth, but he was not going to take any chances with such.

He immediately fell into a crouch and spun around, .45 in hand.

A man stood there.

A man with a rifle.

In that instant Longarm recognized the grocer. The one who said he had no gun. Yeah, right.

Longarm had a gun, and he was a top hand with it. His Colt spat fire and lead.

The grocer's eyes widened in shock, and he staggered backward two tottering paces as a small red stain appeared in the center of his apron bib. The stain spread and flowed as the man's lifeblood drained away until his heart was stopped forever.

He stopped backpedaling, stood upright swaying back and forth for a moment, and then fell facedown into the dirt behind the main street buildings.

He hit hard and made no attempt to soften his fall.

By then Longarm was pressed up against the building where he stood, .45 held at the ready.

When no one else showed himself, Longarm quickly snapped open the loading gate on his Colt and punched out the empty cartridge case. He replaced that one with a fresh round from his pocket, cussing himself for not wearing a filled shell belt like almost everyone else. He just found the damn things heavy and cumbersome. Now he wished he had that inconvenience.

He loaded the sixth chamber too, the one he customarily left empty to avoid an accidental discharge in case he should drop the weapon. Because he was in a business where violence could be sudden and unexpected, he did not drape a safety thong over the hammer to keep the Colt in the leather, and so the empty sixth chamber had always seemed like a sensible alternative.

Now . . . not so much.

Now he wanted that sixth cartridge.

He felt his coat pocket without putting his hand inside again. He could feel the bulge of a meager handful of cartridges in there.

Too much more shooting and the grocer would get his wish, even if not his bounty money.

But then now the poor dead son of a bitch had no use for a king's ransom. He needed to pay no tolls on the road he was taking now.

Reloaded, and .45 still in hand, Longarm resumed his slow progress toward the livery.

Chapter 35

"Oh, shit," Longarm mumbled under his breath. There were two men guarding the livery. Two that he could see. There might well have been more posted inside. It looked like Ed Curen, Sr., was taking no chances that Longarm might get away.

In a way Longarm understood the man's desperation. This whole damn thing had started with something as simple as Ed Junior's arraignment for theft from the mails, which was a federal crime. Thanks to Ed Senior's resistance to solving that so-simple problem, it had escalated until now Senior's own liberty was in jeopardy.

The way things stood now, both father and son were on their way to prison.

Unless Custis Long died.

Of course that would just open another can of worms, because if the Curens succeeded in having Longarm murdered, they would be vulnerable to pretty much every man, woman, and child in Curen Town, any one of whom could go down to Denver and drop a word into Billy Vail's ear. Any one of them could peach on Ed Curen, Sr., and he would be at their mercy from now until Kingdom Come.

Longarm wondered if Ed Senior had thought about that.

By trying to have Longarm killed, he opened himself wide to any kind of blackmail. He would no longer be the ruler in Curen Town. He would be held hostage to everyone else in his own town. His power would be gone. Already was gone, really, just because of his attempts to have Longarm killed, whether he succeeded or not.

And his money might soon be drained away too. The townspeople would soon enough be asking Ed Senior for more. More of almost everything. Especially money, and no man could be wealthy enough to satisfy the desires of the scores of people, possibly hundreds of them, who would be making those demands.

No, Longarm figured that Ed Senior had fucked up badly this time. He wondered if the man realized his error yet.

Funny, it really would have been so simple if only Ed Senior had chosen to give Eddie Junior a stern talking-to and sent him down to Denver for arraignment.

Longarm was fairly sure that the father's influence would have gotten the son off with a slap on the wrist at trial. A little bit of probation. Sentenced to time served even though no real time had been served. Possibly a little community service like picking up road apples on Denver's busy streets.

It could all have gone so well.

But no, Ed Senior wanted it all to go his way. His son should not have to behave like a normal person or be held accountable the way anyone else would. His son was above all that.

Well now it was all crashing down on both father and son, whether or not they succeeded in having Longarm killed before he could get back to Denver to report on what had happened up here. No matter what, the outcome here would not be secret.

Of course that would not help Longarm a whole hell of a lot if he happened to be dead at the time.

He pressed his back against the back wall of one of the main street buildings and pondered what he should do next, how he should go about getting away from a whole town full of people who wanted to collect the bounty placed on his scalp.

Whatever he intended to do next, however, he had better do it pretty damn soon, because he could hear voices approaching somewhere to his right and could see armed guards to his left.

With a building at his back, that left few choices open to him.

Longarm crouched down low and began heading toward the sawmill that lay on the other side of a narrow thread of creek.

Chapter 36

Longarm hunkered down behind a pile of freshly sawed lumber. He paused there for a moment, then removed his Stetson so as to offer a smaller silhouette as he took a look back toward the town.

A group of men—a posse, he supposed—was moving along the back side of the main street buildings. Most of them appeared to be carrying shotguns.

Longarm shuddered. Shotguns made him nervous indeed. It is difficult to miss with a shotgun's wide spread of pellets, and Longarm had an aversion to being shot with anything, but with a shotgun most of all.

The posse of manhunters noisily passed behind the building where Longarm had been standing not five minutes earlier. They went on in the direction of the livery and passed out of his line of sight. He could hear their progress a few moments more and then they were gone.

He pulled back from the edge of the lumber pile and sat, leaning back against the piled boards.

Five thousand dollars bounty, the man had said. Ten years' pay for the average workingman. It was a hell of a lot of money. Enough to make a man do things he normally would not. Enough to make a man contemplate the murder of another.

And enough to share.

Longarm suspected that the posse he'd just seen go past would be only one of many to come.

The men down there would likely form themselves into groups so they could spread out and try to run down and slaughter the threat to Ed Curen, Sr.

He took another cautious look.

There were men guarding the livery. More than he'd at first thought. They reasoned, correctly, that his first thought would be to want a way to get out of Curen Town and head either down to Manitou or out to Fairplay.

Apparently all the livestock in town had been rounded up and put under guard in the livery barn and the adjacent corrals.

Longarm decided his best chance would be to lie low until nightfall, then try to steal an animal.

That decision made, he relaxed.

Too soon, as it happened.

"It's him!" the shout rose. "Come quick, boys, it's him for sure, there by that stack of lumber."

Longarm shot to his feet, heart pounding and lungs panting for breath that suddenly did not want to come.

"Come on, boys, let's get him."

Longarm began to run.

Chapter 37

He was beginning to feel like a rabbit with a pack of hounds on its trail.

Except, dammit, he had always thought of himself as more of a fox than a rabbit. It was not his way to hide from trouble, not even against long odds.

The problem here was that even if he had had plenty of ammunition, he really did not want to go around shooting down the innocent citizens of Curen Town.

Well, innocent except for their desire to commit murder. There was that against them.

Even so, the fault lay with Edward Curen, Sr., and his five-thousand-dollar bounty.

Five thousand dollars. Ten years' pay. The numbers kept running through his mind. He could understand how that much money would tempt a man past his normal store of morals and decency. If the son of a bitch had any morals and decency, that is. It seemed that a fair amount of the population here was lacking in those qualities.

And so, going against his usual inclinations, Longarm found a warren deep in the underbrush and settled in to wait for the darkness that could hide and protect him.

At least, he thought, the condemned man had been

permitted a hefty last meal. The problem, on the other hand, was that that last meal might have to last him awhile. He could not waltz into the café now and order supper. Nor that picnic basket filled with food. It would have come in handy about now, he thought.

He lay half-covered in dead leafs and sprawling juniper fans.

Twice he heard the approach of footsteps and prepared for a last-ditch fight, only to discover that the noise was caused by browsing elk. The creatures sounded just like a band of humans moving slowly, as if stalking something. Or someone.

The elk were surprisingly loud when they were unmolested and unsuspicious about their surroundings. Longarm knew, though, that if they were to catch his scent, they could move away as silently as wisps of ground fog, quiet as the proverbial ghosts.

These were all cows and half-grown calves. The calves were as big as Texas range steers, but without the horns, and would have provided even better meat than a tough Texas steer.

This was not, however, a very good time to be thinking about food.

Longarm closed his eyes and willed himself to get some sleep.

He might well need that rest come nightfall.

Chapter 38

There was no moon, but there was no cloud cover either, and the starlight at this elevation was practically bright enough to read by. Longarm's best hope was that the men in town would be indoors with lighted lamps and therefore with little to no night vision.

He slipped down the hill where he had been holed up throughout the daylight hours and headed once again for the livery.

As he had more than half expected, the barn and the corrals too were still being heavily guarded. And those men were *not* close to lamps that would reduce their night vision.

He had not really expected to be able to steal a horse. But it would have been nice, and it was only sensible to take a look.

Well, he had taken that look, and nothing had come of it. Now he knew. Now he could put that out of mind, at least for the time being. If things changed, he could take another look then, but for right now there was no point in risking death or capture, and he was certain that capture in this case would have exactly the same result as being gunned down by a dozen shotgun blasts. Ed Curen would not permit him to leave Curen Town alive if the man ever got his hands on Longarm.

Satisfied that the livery was all too well guarded, he worked his way around it, sticking to the deepest shadows wherever possible.

He crossed over to the other side of town and through an alley so he could work his way up behind the line of businesses on that side of the main street.

The rented doctor buggy was still parked on the street where he had left it. With any kind of luck his carpetbag would still be behind the seat, and in that were both the telegraph key that he always carried and, almost as valuable, his spare .45 cartridges.

He passed behind the business buildings almost to the end of the block, then squeezed through another narrow alleyway to return to the street.

He emerged about thirty feet from the buggy.

Light and noise streamed from the several saloons nearby, and there were lamps in several windows along the street as well.

In case someone might be looking out of one of those windows, Longarm tugged his Stetson low to partially cover his face and sauntered just as casually as he could manage out to the dark and silent buggy. He got to it quickly and could not help but glance furtively up and down the street.

No one seemed to be paying any attention.

He turned to the buggy again and reached in behind the seat.

Nothing! His carpetbag was not there.

Chapter 39

A door opened nearby and a shaft of lamplight spilled out onto the boards of the sidewalk.

Longarm could hear voices. Men talking. Which meant more than one man would likely emerge onto the sidewalk. Which meant the likelihood of him being discovered was high. He was crouched beside the doctor buggy, in plain view from that side of the vehicle.

He did the only thing he could think of at that moment. He crawled into the footwell of the rig, insinuating himself on hands and knees between the seat and the dashboard.

He had never noticed before, at least not to really pay attention, how much grit and grime were left on the floor of a driving rig. Now he was on all fours inside the buggy, and he felt the distinct need to wash his hands of the grit that cut into his palms.

On the other hand it was considerably better to have bits of gravel and mud cut into his hands than to have a flight of double-ought buckshot and .45 slugs cutting into his belly. He had no doubt that that was exactly what would happen if he were discovered on the streets of Curen Town. Better by far to put up with the gravel that was digging into his palms.

He crouched there, silent, while not ten feet away some

asshole was bragging about "Just let me get a look at him, Tom. Just a glimpse, that's all. I got my old gun here loaded with goose loads. That oughta bring down any son of a bitch."

"You know that he's a deputy U.S. marshal, don't you, Harry?"

"What I know is that he's worth five thousand U.S. dollars, dead or alive. What I know is what I'd do for that kind of money, Tom. Are you saying that you wouldn't?"

In a softer, calmer voice than Harry's, Tom said, "There's no amount of money that would make me volunteer to think of myself as a murderer. That's the sort of thing, just knowing it his own self, that would stick with a man his whole life through, even if he got away with it."

"Well if we happen to see the bastard, don't get in my way while I gun him down."

"That's exactly what I mean when I say murder, Harry. You don't know the facts here. You certainly don't know that Ed is in the right, nor what this marshal did to make Ed put the bounty on him."

"All I need to know is five thousand dollars. That's plenty cause as far as I'm concerned," Harry insisted.

The men walked on, their voices growing fainter until Longarm could no longer hear their conversation.

Hurray for Tom, Longarm thought bitterly.

Then his lips thinned into something approaching a smile, if a sarcastic one, as he thought of the old saw about the Texas Rangers. One Ranger per mob. Well it was just a damned shame that that old Ranger William Vail was not here to take over and prove that adage. Let Billy use his magical powers to overcome the situation in Curen Town, and they could all go home safe and happy.

But by God with both Ed Curen, Sr., and Eddie Curen, Jr., in handcuffs and headed for the hoosgow.

Longarm snapped his fingers. Aloud. And winced slightly at the noise after he did so. It was just a damned good thing there was no one passing close by at the moment to overhear.

His response, though, was to thinking about jail.

Curen Town had a jail. The town also had a marshal who paid scant attention to either position or place. It was very likely that the town marshal's office would be empty at this hour.

Longarm permitted himself a smile as he cautiously rose up enough so he could see over the dashboard and check whether there were any townspeople close by.

There were none, so he backed slowly out of the buggy and to the ground. Once there, he stood tall, completely exposed but knowing that if he tried to be overly furtive when he was there in plain sight, he would only call undue attention to himself.

Better to act like any after-work reveler on his way home after a round or two.

Longarm stuck his hands into his pockets and sashayed down the street in the direction of Seth Greenwald's office.

Chapter 40

Longarm nearly laughed out loud. The windows in the Curen Town jail were heavily barred with thick slabs of iron interlaced together. No one could break in or out without first making noise shattering the glass window and then spending some hours trying to saw through the bars.

Yet between those wonderfully secure front windows was a door that had a cheap and mail order lock on it.

Longarm actually did chuckle as he took out his pocketknife, opened it, and quickly jimmied the door lock. He probably had the door open as quickly—or more so—than if he had had a key.

He stepped inside and shut the door behind him.

Once inside, he opened Greenwald's desk and went through the drawers.

He found a pint bottle of whiskey in the first drawer he opened. The bottle had about an inch of cheap whiskey in it. Longarm pulled the cork and finished it off. Then, grinning, he put the cork back into the bottle and returned the bottle to the drawer where he had found it. He wondered if Seth Greenwald would figure out what had happened to his hooch.

Whiskey, nice though it was, was not what he had come here for.

There was a gun rack screwed onto the side wall to the left, behind Greenwald's desk. The rack was empty, although Longarm was sure he had seen guns in it the last time he was in the office.

That probably accounted for a good many of the guns that were floating around town right now as part of the search to find and to murder the U.S. deputy.

A rifle in his own hands would have been nice, but what was important at the moment was that he found two boxes of .45 cartridges in a bottom drawer in the marshal's desk.

Longarm confiscated both of them. He broke open one box and dropped a handful of the squat, lead-tipped cartridges into his right-hand coat pocket. The remainder of that box and the complete second box went into a canvas bag that had been intended for . . . who the hell knew. Longarm did not have a clue. And did not care.

From his point of view the important thing was that the bag had a wide canvas strap attached for carrying over the shoulder. He draped the bag, heavy with a box and a half of .45s, over his shoulder so it hung on his left side, leaving the right with free access to the loose cartridges in his pocket.

With all that firepower, he figured he *could* slaughter half the damn town if he had to.

But "could" and "would" were two entirely different animals. He still hoped he could make his arrests and get out of here without having to kill any more townspeople.

He checked quickly around the rest of the office but came up with nothing that would be useful.

What he really needed now, he thought, was a telegraph line. Or at the least a telegraph key. He could climb a pole and tap into a wire if he had to, but one way or another he needed a key if he wanted to get a message out to One Ranger/One Mob Billy Vail.

Longarm peered out to make sure the street was clear at the moment, then stepped out onto the sidewalk.

Chapter 41

Behind him!

Longarm whirled, Colt in hand.

Something moved at the corner of the building, and he nearly triggered off a round. Barely in time he held his fire. The sound, the movement were caused by some small animal—a cat or a raccoon perhaps—rummaging in the trash.

Longarm took a deep breath and returned the .45 to its leather. Apparently this business of having an entire town after his scalp was beginning to spook him. What he needed, he realized, was to calm down and do what had to be done. That was the way he had always done things, one bite of the apple at a time. And always within the law.

He grinned silently to himself and admitted that, well, if not entirely within the letter of the law, then certainly within its spirit.

But for the Curens father and son, damn them, he wanted—intended—to apply the full letter of the law, Ed for the attempted murder of a federal officer and Eddie for theft from the mails.

Of course just like in the old trapper's recipe for cooking rabbit stew, first catch the rabbit.

In this case it was a matter of first "catching" Ed Curen, Sr. If the father was down in Denver behind bars, everything else would fall into place. There would no longer be any reason for the people here to want Longarm dead. There would no longer be the boss of the town to command that job or to pay for its completion.

With no incentive for that hired murder, the guns of Curen Town would go back into the closets, and Longarm would no longer have to worry about assassins lurking in the shadows.

For the time being, though, he damned well better worry about that, because half the town or more seemed to be salivating for the five-thousand-dollar reward that Ed Curen had posted on Custis Long's head.

Longarm shuddered thinking about it, and headed for the post office building.

He was not sure exactly where the telegraph station was here in town, but the post office was a reasonable place to start looking.

Chapter 42

The Curen Town post office was a separate building standing on a street corner. It was small, built of the locally milled planks that nearly all the town's buildings were. It also, Longarm was pleased to discover, had a back door.

The latch yielded easily to Longarm's pocketknife, and he slipped inside without, he hoped, being seen from the side street.

Once inside, he wished he could light a lamp or at least strike a match, but either of those could be seen through the front windows, and that could lead to more gunfire. And to someone's death. He did not want that, not his or anyone else's, not even Ed Curen's.

He quickly rummaged through the area behind the customer counter. There was, unfortunately, no telegraph inside the post office.

The stagecoach stop, if he remembered correctly, was a general mercantile on a side street two blocks down. Logic suggested that could also be the telegraph office.

Cussing under his breath, Longarm let himself out of the post office and headed through an alley that led behind it in the direction of the mercantile.

On the other side of the line of main street buildings he

could hear music and laughter despite the late hour. But then the men of Curen Town had been having themselves something of a holiday, getting off work early to go on a manhunt. It sounded like they were enjoying themselves.

"Bastards," Longarm muttered softly to himself. Hunting an innocent man for money was such fun! Better even than hunting elk.

Except this quarry could shoot back if it had to, damn them. And would. If he had to. He sighed and shook his head, feeling suddenly weary.

He checked in the sheds and small barns located behind the business structures. Normally one would expect to find some animals there. Dray horses if nothing else. Now . . . nothing. It seemed that every horse and mule in town had been packed into the livery and its corrals and put under close guard, in an obvious attempt to keep him from getting hold of one.

Unfortunately that plan was working. He found plenty of locally cut hay in those sheds but no animals.

Still, he checked each one as he came to it. Then moved on.

If he could just get his hands on a telegraph key, he could send a message to Billy asking for help. Under the circumstances, he was not too proud to ask for help.

If he could just get to the telegraph.

Chapter 43

"Halt! Who goes there?"

The voice was crisp and strong. A former soldier, no doubt. A former soldier with respect for the law? That was the question.

Longarm froze in place. He could not know if the soldier had already seen him or only heard his footsteps.

The good thing was that the man had not fired at him.

And that suggested that perhaps, just perhaps, the soldier indeed had *not* seen him yet and did not know where to aim.

In a very low voice Longarm answered, "Deputy U.S. Marshal Custis Long. Who are you?"

"I been posted to guard this place."

"Oh? Why?" Longarm said.

"The telegraph. It's inside."

Which told Longarm where the man was as well as why he was there. He should have known that Curen would not allow such a tempting target as that telegraph key to go unguarded.

"I understand that, but why are you doing this?" Longarm asked. "Why would you take up arms against a federal lawman? Don't you know you could be charged with insurrection?"

He heard a chuckle in the night. He thought it came from the shadows behind the harness maker's shop. That would be next door to the mercantile where he suspected the telegraph would be.

"Marshal, I been charged with insurrection before this. Guilty of it too, by Godfrey."

"Johnny Reb, eh?"

"From the first to the last and in my heart always will be. What about you, Marshal?"

"Oh, I was there," Longarm said.

"Which side?"

"Does it matter?"

There was a pause, then the guard said, "I suppose it doesn't after this much time. If you've let it go, who am I to say you're wrong?"

"You still haven't told me why here, why now," Longarm said.

"A hundred dollars in gold for each and every night," the man answered. He chuckled again. "That's a hell of a lot more than I used to make for a night on guard duty."

"Aye, I hear that. I don't suppose you'd stand clear and let me in there. I am the law here, you know. Not him. It'd be the right thing to do."

Longarm was pretty sure he had the man spotted now. An even darker shadow within a dark shadow, standing in the slightly recessed rear doorway of the harness maker's shop.

"I took the man's money," the guard responded.

Longarm sighed. He could easily kill the soldier.

He did not want to do that.

This man had done no wrong. Oh, perhaps technically speaking he could be considered guilty of insurrection, taking up arms against the duly constituted authority.

But, dammit, he had done no wrong. Not the way Custis Long thought of things, he had not.

And he did not deserve to die taking an honorable stand.

He had accepted Edward Curen's money and so felt obligated to carry through with the job regardless of the law's fine-tipped letter.

No, there was no way Longarm could gun down a man like that.

"In that case, Reb, I'll wish you a pleasant good night an' be on my way."

"Good night, Marshal." The soldier laughed. "Mind you don't step on that rake some kid left lying in the dirt behind you. It could fly up and give you a nasty bump."

Longarm looked down and behind him. Damned if there wasn't a rake lying there. So the soldier had known where he was all along, or at least had figured it out, just as Longarm had spotted him in the shadows.

"G'night, Reb."

"Good night, Marshal. Godspeed."

Chapter 44

Longarm would have been proud to stand up to a bar beside that man and buy him a drink. There was no way he wanted to shoot him.

Sometimes life just deals you a lousy hand, he reflected.

But then it is not the cards you are given but what you do with them that counts.

He took a moment to orient himself, then peered off toward the east. The sky there was perhaps a little grayer than it had been, a little lighter. This was a false dawn, but the real thing would be along before too long. Longarm knew he had to get out of the streets and the alleys of Curen Town before that happened. It seemed he had waited a little too long before setting out this evening.

Of course he had not known the obstacles he would run into.

No horse. No telegraph. So . . . what?

He did not know anyone in town he could turn to, no one he could count as a friend.

He smiled. No one short of that Johnny Reb guard back there, and that man would shoot him if he had to.

Longarm had no intention of forcing the Reb to do that.

The only other person . . .

He stopped. And laughed, barely able to keep the sound contained.

Of course there was someone he could turn to now.

Again he oriented himself in the back alleys of Curen Town.

Then, resolute on what needed to be done, he set off at a brisk pace to take advantage of the night as long as he could.

Chapter 45

The front door was in plain view of too many neighbors, and daylight was swiftly approaching. Worse, he was beginning to see lamp light behind windows in nearby houses.

Two houses down he heard the slap of a spring-loaded screen door as someone went out the back, likely to a shitter.

Longarm had intended to go in the front. Instead he changed his plan and worked his way around to the back, over a fence and onto the back porch.

The door was bolted from the inside and would not yield to his attempts to jimmy it, so he dropped down from the porch and went to a back window instead. The screen panel on that opening did give way to his probing knife. He slipped the latch easily, prized the screen out of the way, and tried the window.

The window proved to be unlocked and gave easily to his efforts to lift it.

Longarm could hear a pair of sash weights rattle as they did their job keeping the heavy window frame from falling back down again. He smiled, pressed his palms down on the windowsill, and boosted himself inside.

He found himself in a bedroom. An occupied bedroom.

The room was nearly dark, but morning light was beginning to seep in through the open window. He could easily see a mass of jet-black hair lying stark against the white of a pillowcase.

The bedcovers were pulled up to the girl's neck, but Longarm already knew what lay beneath them.

He wondered . . .

He walked softly over to the bedside and knelt beside the bed. He slipped a hand beneath the sheets.

And smiled.

She did indeed sleep naked. He was not surprised.

Longarm pulled his hand back and moved to the head of the bed. He leaned down and brushed a wisp of hair off her face, then gently kissed her on the lips.

Her eyes opened—violet, he decided now—and she smiled.

"Good morning, dear. I thought everyone was out to kill you. I take it they failed."

"So far," he said, "but you can help to make that a permanent sort o' thing."

"And just why would I want to do that, dear?" Rebecca Thorn asked.

"Oh, for a couple reasons," Longarm said. "One is that you're just crazy 'bout me. Another is 'cause if anything does happen to me, other deputies will come to see. Eddie and his father will both go to prison, and as an accessory you could wind up there too." He smiled and kissed her again. "'Specially since I wouldn't be around to speak in your defense, y'see. But if you help me, I can make sure you ain't charged with anything." This time there were some tongues involved in what proved to be more than a quick kiss.

Of course the truth was that Rebecca was in no danger of being charged with any crime and would not be no matter what happened to Longarm. But he seriously doubted that she knew enough about the law to understand that.

And anyway he had not lied. Exactly. He had said she *could* be charged with a crime, not that she *would* be.

"You would make sure nothing happens to me, lover?" she whispered, her hand sliding down toward his crotch.

"Uh-huh. I could guarantee it."

"Then I think you should get out of those clothes and get in here with me," Rebecca said, sweeping the covers aside for his entry.

His entry into the bed, and into Rebecca too.

Chapter 46

Rebecca placed her hand lightly on Longarm's chest, guiding him down onto his back. She bent down over him, her nipples teasing his chest while she kissed him.

Pulling back from the kiss, she moved down and inserted herself between his legs. With one hand she fondled his balls, while the other stroked his cock.

"You have a beautiful dick," she said. "Has anybody ever told you that? It isn't just big, it is beautiful."

Rebecca bent lower, teasing his cock, brushing her lips lightly over it. Then the tip of her tongue. Finally she peeled back his foreskin, parted her lips, and took him into her mouth.

"Ah, hot, hot," he muttered.

"Mmm."

He began to laugh, but Rebecca did not seem to mind. She kept on sucking.

Longarm reached down and gently stroked the back of her head while the girl continued to suck his cock and fondle his balls.

After a few moments she pulled away from him enough so she could speak. "Would you like to come in my mouth?" she asked.

"Would you like for me to?" Longarm said.

Rebecca laughed and squeezed his prick. "Yes. I'd like that, I think." Impishly, she added, "The first time, that is."

"And the second time?" he asked.

"Oh, you know where I want that," she said. "But I don't want to be knocked up. Not anymore, I don't, not now that Eddie isn't the great catch that I thought he would be."

"Lucky, then, that you didn't get pregnant," Longarm said.

She giggled. "That's the nice thing about blow jobs. A girl can't get pregnant from the cum she swallows. Besides, I like to do it. I like the taste of it and the way a dick feels in my mouth."

"Speaking of which . . ."

"I haven't forgotten," she said. "Just taking a break."

She dipped her head and teased him for a moment, her breath cool on flesh that was wet with her saliva. Then again she parted her lips and took him fully into the heat of her mouth.

Longarm lay back and let the girl suck him.

Chapter 47

Longarm woke up with a start. Rebecca was lying beside him, watching him as he slept. She smiled when she saw that he was awake.

"Hello," she said. "You dropped off for a few minutes there."

"That'd be 'cause you wore me out."

"You're complaining?"

"Not hardly," he said. "I can't think of a better way to get that way." He grinned. "You do know how to relax a man."

"No complaints?" she asked.

"No complaints," he said.

"Are you hungry?"

"I could eat," Longarm told her. At the thought of food his stomach rumbled.

Rebecca laughed and sat up. "I'll fix us some breakfast. Stay there and get some more sleep if you like."

"Thanks, but I'll get up too." Longarm swung his legs off the side of the bed and sat up. He rubbed his eyes and swept a hand over his hair to smooth it down. He fingered his chin. He needed a shave, but that would just have to wait, as his razor was in the carpetbag—wherever that was now—and he was in no position to walk into the barber's.

Rebecca pulled on a robe and disappeared toward the kitchen. Longarm heard the clang of the stove's firebox door as he was getting dressed. By the time he joined her in the kitchen, Rebecca had a pot of coffee heating and was busy mixing batter in a large bowl.

"Bacon and biscuits be all right for breakfast?" she asked.

"Fine."

"Sit down," she said. "The coffee is left over from last night, but it should still be good. It will be hot in a minute or two."

"Thanks." He pulled out a chair and sat at the kitchen table.

"You can stay here," she said. "In a few days they will think you've gotten away from them and quit looking so hard."

"That's nice o' you, girl, but if you're willin' to help, I have something else in mind."

"You meant what you said?" she asked. "About making sure I don't get in trouble with the law, I mean?"

Longarm nodded. "I meant that. You won't be charged with anything."

"Then I'll help you any way I can," Rebecca promised. "Just tell me what you want me to do and I'll do it."

Longarm smiled. "First off, I'd sure like to have that cup o' coffee and a bite o' something to eat. Then, well, there's a way you could help me plenty."

"Whatever you want," she said. She set the mixing bowl aside and began to grease a baking pan for the biscuits.

He could be making the worst mistake of his life, Longarm thought. And the very last one. But . . . he didn't think so. He was fairly sure he could trust Rebecca to do what he asked of her, just so long as she thought that helping him was in her own best interests.

She laid a finger against the side of the coffeepot, decided it was hot enough, and poured a cup for Longarm and another for herself; then she slid the pan of biscuits into the oven and began slicing bacon into a skillet.

The condemned man, Longarm mused, was fixing to eat a hearty meal.

After that . . . it would all depend on Rebecca and her willingness to help.

Or to betray him so Edward Curen could pay out that bounty on Longarm's head.

Chapter 48

He could hear the voices approaching the front of Rebecca's house, voices light and laughing.

Longarm's lips thinned in a tight, satisfied smile. Come right in, said the spider to the fly, he thought with satisfaction.

Of course he was still not quite positive about Rebecca. She could well be betraying him. Or helping him.

He would know which in just another minute or so.

The front door opened and he could hear Rebecca's voice sounding light and happy. He could hear another voice too, this one deeper, masculine.

Only one man's voice. That was good. Apparently there was no posse coming to take him to Ed Senior

"Come into the bedroom, dear," Rebecca said. "I have something in there to show you."

"Really? Something new?" the man asked.

"Yes, I think you could say that," she said. "Come on now."

"Can I have a drink first?"

"In the bedroom," she insisted.

"If you say so."

Their footsteps approached the bedroom, where Longarm was standing beside Rebecca's wardrobe, his .45 in hand.

"Now, what is this new thing you have?" the man was asking as he stepped into the bedroom.

"Oh, shit!" he groaned as Longarm stepped out into the open and placed the muzzle of his revolver under the startled fellow's nose.

"Good morning, Eddie," Longarm said.

Ed Curen, Jr., stood stiff and still, but that did not stop him from hissing, "You bitch. You fucking bitch."

"Careful what you say, Eddie. The lady is under my protection."

"Lady? She's nothing but a bitch. A Judas, that's what she is," Curen snapped.

"Turn around, Eddie. Put your hands behind you."

"Or what?" Eddie demanded.

Longarm shrugged. "Or I buffalo you with this Colt and put the cuffs on you while you're on the floor."

Eddie Curen was belligerent, but he was not brave and he did not want to be hit. He turned, as Longarm asked, and put both hands behind him while Longarm secured the handcuffs in place.

"They're too tight," Eddie whined. "Rebecca? Where'd the bitch go?"

"Sit down, Eddie. Rebecca will be back in a minute," Longarm said.

He was right about that. She appeared moments later carrying a cup of fresh coffee for Longarm. "All right?" she asked. "Did I do good?"

"You did good, honey," he said.

"You'll tell the judge that, right?"

"Absolutely," he promised. "Just like I said I would."

"Is there anything else?" she asked.

"You can go to hell," Eddie injected into the conversation. "You can go straight to hell, you bitch."

Longarm jabbed him over the kidney with the muzzle of

his .45. "Shut up, Eddie. Rebecca is assisting a deputy United States marshal. And you, kid, are a prisoner of the same. So shut the fuck up. Now sit and be quiet." He turned to Rebecca and nodded.

"Now?" she asked.

"Sure," Longarm told her. "There's no point in waitin' for it."

"All right, but I'm scared."

"There's nothin' to be scared of."

"They could . . . I don't know. Shoot me or . . . or who knows what." She shuddered. "I don't trust them."

"Hell, you shouldn't ought to trust them. Of course you can't trust them, but you don't have to. Just do what I told you, then get out of sight and stay there."

"How will I know . . . ?"

"Oh, I'm pretty sure you'll know when this is all over and it's safe for you to come out again. Go on now," Longarm said. He gave Rebecca a kiss and a friendly slap on the ass and sent her on her way.

"Where's the bitch going?" Eddie asked.

"You'll see quick enough what she's doing," Longarm told him. "So just set there an' be quiet so's I don't have t' hurt you."

"You can't do that," Eddie insisted. "It's against the rules. Isn't it?"

Longarm chuckled. "Yup. It's completely against the rules for a prisoner to be beat while he's in custody." The chuckle turned into laughter. "But maybe you've heard that prisoners can fall down an' hurt themselves. Hurt themselves bad sometimes."

"You wouldn't dare. My father . . ." Eddie began. Then comprehension seemed to reach him, and his voice tailed away into silence. "Oh," he said after another moment.

"Exactly," Longarm said. He tucked Eddie's Remington revolver behind his belt, took Eddie by the arm, and led him out into the parlor. "Now we'll both set an' wait," he said.

Chapter 49

"Outside," Longarm ordered. He prodded Eddie in the back using the muzzle of his Colt for emphasis.

"Right out in the open?" Eddie asked.

"Exactly," Longarm said. "You wouldn't want somebody shooting any which way, would you? Why, you might get shot by mistake. By your very own friends. Oh, that's right. You don't have friends, you just have toadies who want to have your daddy's goodwill. Doesn't matter. You wouldn't want to get shot by any o' them neither, I'd guess."

Eddie nudged the door open with an elbow and stepped out onto the front porch, Longarm close behind him.

"Sit in that chair there," Longarm ordered. "No, the straight chair. I'll be takin' the wicker rocking chair for m'self if you please."

"Yes, sir." Eddie Curen, Jr., was decidedly subdued now at the thought of what could happen to him, either at Custis Long's hands or those of the possibly excited townspeople who wanted to collect the bounty on Longarm's scalp.

"Y'know, Eddie, this is probably the first time in your life that your daddy's protection don't mean shit," Longarm mused. "The experience might be good for you, at that."

"Going to prison could be good for me?" Eddie said.

"It beats bein' dead. Beats the sentence your father is lookin' at too. He'll be in three, four times as long as you will," Longarm said.

Eddie's head snapped around and he stared hard at Longarm for a moment. "He won't . . . You wouldn't . . ."

"Yes, I would, Eddie, and yes, I will. Your daddy has attempted to take the life of a federal lawman. No judge down there will look light at that. You, you'll get off easy. Might've got off with nothing more'n probation if you'd gone with me to begin with and fought it through lawyer Wilson. You've gone past that now, of course."

"But my father," Eddie said. "What about him?"

"Attempted murder, he's likely looking at ten, fifteen years in a federal penitentiary. Leavenworth or one o' them."

Eddie shook his head. "He won't allow that to happen, Marshal. I know him. He won't let you take him in."

"Me or somebody that comes after me, kid. There's more of us than there is o' him, and we're meaner. The law won't quit until he's paid the price. Sorry, but that's just the way things are."

Eddie smirked and pointed with his chin. "You're in for it now, Marshal. My friends are coming to get me now."

"I see 'em, kid." Longarm yawned—it was tension rather than sleepiness that caused it—and pressed the muzzle of his .45 into Eddie's ribs. "Just so you know, kid, I'll pull the trigger on you if I'm going under, and there ain't any amount of bullets can put me down so quick that I won't."

A mob of townspeople were coming close now, all of them armed, probably all of them with visions of that reward money floating through their minds.

"Now, kid, let's see if your daddy is willin' to risk you dying just so he can take me down."

Chapter 50

Longarm turned his attention to the mob of fifty or sixty men. He kept his .45 pressed against Eddie's side and raised his voice. "That's far enough, boys. You can see plain enough that I got my pistol tight against Eddie. Does one o' you shoot me . . . which you can easily do from there . . . then I shoot too. If I'm shot, Eddie dies. And how d'you think Ed Senior will like that, eh? Likely not a helluva lot, so hold your water an' talk to his old man before you decide to do anything."

"Don't listen to him," some hothead in the crowd yelled. "We can all shoot at once. Put one in his head. That would do for him."

"The man is right," Longarm shot back in a loud but calm voice. "You could all take close aim and all shoot at once. Why, you'd blow my head clean off. Bust it open like a watermelon dropped on a rock. The thing is, my dyin' twitch would be enough to make this here pistol go off. Then both me and Eddie here would be dead. You think Ed Senior would pay a reward to somebody that got his boy killed? Put your minds to it an' see what you come up with about that. Do that before you decide to gang up an' shoot me."

Longarm reached rather awkwardly inside his coat with

his left hand, the right being occupied with Eddie and the .45, and pulled out a cheroot. He nipped the twist off with his teeth and spat the bit of tobacco out, then dipped two fingers of his left hand into a vest pocket to bring out a match.

He crossed his legs and scraped the match aflame on the sole of his boot and lighted the cheroot.

He held the cheroot between his teeth and smiled—it came across as more of a grimace than a smile—at the crowd while he drew Eddie's Remington from his waistband, again using his left hand.

In a loud, clear voice he said, "I'm not near as good with a shooter left-handed, but I'm betting I can hit somewhere in the bunch o' you assholes with this, um, with this here whatever it is. I dunno. Maybe a .45. Or could be a .44-40. Something like that. For sure something big enough to put a hurtin' on somebody. Maybe even two o' you if the cartridge is powerful enough to go clear through the first one I hit an' do in whoever is behind him.

"The thing is, I think in just a minute or two here I'm gonna shoot into you all. The bunch o' you standin' there, wantin' to kill me and collect blood money, that pisses me off, boys. What makes it all the worse is that you idiots are right out in public, threatenin' the life of a deputy United States marshal, and none o' you stoppin' to think that by doin' it you are risking probably a ten- to fifteen-year stretch in Leavenworth.

"With that in mind, I'm gonna start fixin' your faces in my mind so that if I live to get out of this jam, I can testify before a federal judge about who'all it was as threatened me with death or bodily harm. So you think about that, an' while you are thinkin', I'd suggest that someone go fetch Ed Curen. Tell him if he wants his boy to survive this day, he'd best get his sorry ass over here and surrender himself to me. And he'd best do it pronto."

Longarm laid the Remington in his lap while he took a deep drag on the cheroot and puffed out some smoke rings.

There was a buzz of whispered murmurings within the crowd and then one by one the townspeople started drifting away, until only a handful remained.

Longarm wished to hell the rest would go too. His wrist was beginning to get tired from holding the heavy Colt on Eddie.

There was no way he intended to let that show to those miserable sons of bitches who were still standing in front of him, however.

He puffed on the cheroot a little more, tapped the ash off, and stuck it back between his teeth. He picked up the Remington again and pointed it in the general direction of the men standing in front of him.

If the bastards called his bluff and he had to start shooting, there was going to be a real bloodbath here, and he did not want that.

He would do it, though, if he had to, and he was *not* going down alone, dammit.

"Here he comes, boys, here he comes," someone shouted.

Good, Longarm thought. Things were about to get better now.

Or they were going to get much, much worse.

Chapter 51

Ed Curen, Sr., must have been working underground. Well, inspecting underground. Longarm doubted that the great man did much in the way of manual labor. He had minions for that.

He showed up dressed in a flannel shirt, denim trousers held up with canvas suspenders, a cloth cap, and knee-high rubber boots. As far as Longarm could see, he did not appear to be armed. But then he had minions for that too.

"Hello, Ed," Longarm said when Curen was close enough to chat. "Come to do the job yourself an' save five grand, have you?"

"What do you think you are doing with my boy there, Long?" Curen demanded.

"I think I'm arresting him, Ed. After that I think I'll arrest you too." Longarm grinned and tapped the ash off his cheroot, returned it to his teeth, and again picked up the Remington.

"You'll play hell doing either," Curen growled.

Longarm shrugged. "Have it your way, but I might ought to mention that my hand is getting mighty weary. Before too awful long I'm gonna decide to make a break outa this town. I reckon I'll have to shoot my way out an' I got to be honest with you, Ed. If I don't think I can take Eddie with me, I'll shoot him right here an' leave him layin' on this here porch."

Curen turned pale. He whirled and barked, "Whit. Hand me your rifle."

A man standing nearby surrendered his weapon, which was probably one that had come from the town marshal's office anyway.

Curen started to turn back toward Longarm, who said, "I'll give you the same speech I gave to these other boys. The deal is, you can shoot me dead as last fall's hog, but if you do, my finger will trip the trigger on this hair-trigger Colt o' mine and a .45 slug will drive through your boy's short ribs and on through his guts. Won't be no doctor alive can bring a man back from something like that."

Longarm hoped the senior Curen had not soldiered in the recent unpleasantness or in the Indian wars afterward. If he had, he likely had seen men survive the most awful wounds, things even the doctors could not understand, beyond muttering that it just was not their time to go and so they stayed against all odds.

On the other hand, even if Curen had soldiered in his youth, he would not want to trust his boy's life to that slim chance. Or so Longarm reasoned.

"What do you want, Long?" Curen said in a controlled voice, the man's fury barely contained.

Longarm took his time with another drag on the cheroot then flicked the butt out into Rebecca's yard. "I want shut o' Curen Town," he said. "Me and your boy. I want that doctor buggy that I came in and the mule to pull it. And I want you to withdraw that offer of five thousand bounty, so's me and Eddie can have us a nice, unexciting drive down to Manitou."

Even if—big if—Curen agreed to let them leave the town, Longarm had no illusions that the townsfolk would just wave good-bye and let them go. If he could convince them that he was headed down to Manitou by way of the old Ute track, well, so much the better.

They would figure it out soon enough that he was driving over to Fairplay instead, but any kind of a lead on the pack would be a help. If his luck really ran strong, Curen might divide his forces and send some to Manitou and some to Fairplay.

That at least would cut down the odds a little.

Longarm was willing to take what little he could get if it gave him just that much better a chance to get out of this deal alive.

"What d'you think, Ed?"

Curen nodded. "The buggy. The mule. And no interference along the way."

Longarm did not believe that last part for half a heartbeat, but he was willing to take what he could get.

Curen spun on his heels and started to stalk away. He stopped suddenly, whirled, and said, "Be ready, Eddie. Whatever happens, you be ready."

"Yes, Papa. I will be."

"Oh, yes," Longarm called. "I want two more things. A sawed-off twelve-gauge . . . with shells, of course . . . and a roll of bundling wire."

"Wire?" Curen said, eyebrows rising.

"That's right. A roll o' light wire."

"What size shot in those shells?" Curen asked.

"That don't matter, mister. At the range I'd be shooting, blank shells would do as good as double-ought buck."

Curen looked like he would pass out. "You . . . you wouldn't, you bastard."

"Oh, but I would," Longarm assured him. He smiled wickedly. "It'd take the boy's head plumb off, wouldn't it."

"You *bastard*!" the distraught father screamed.

Longarm nodded. Smiled again. "That's right, I am. So see to it that nothin' happens to me. I can promise you one thing though. After I get Eddie safe in Denver, I'll be comin' back up here for you, Ed. You have my word on it."

Curen spun on his heels and stomped away and out of sight.

"Come along, Eddie," Longarm said. "Let's us go in an' see can we find somethin' to eat in the little lady's kitchen."

Chapter 52

Curen sent a minion. Longarm was standing in Rebecca's foyer, watching through the screen door. The shotgun and a canvas sack, presumably containing the shells and the wire, were brought by a tall, gangly youngster with red hair and a butcher's apron, complete with blood.

Without opening the screen, Longarm said, "Put those down on the chair there, son, an' take off that apron. I wouldn't want to think you was hiding anything under it."

"I'm not, sir, I . . . I . . ."

"It's all right, kid. I'm not gonna shoot you without I have to, an' even then I'd shoot Eddie first just to make sure there ain't no mistakes."

"Yes, sir." The boy laid the shotgun down on the chair where Longarm indicated and placed the bag beside it. "Is there anything else, sir?"

"No, you done your job. Take off now." He did not have to say it twice. The young man bounded off the porch and out through the gate fast as any jackrabbit Longarm had ever seen.

"Come with me," Longarm said, prodding Eddie in the ribs.

"That hurts, you know," the younger Curen protested.

"Not near as much as if I pull the trigger. Now, come along nice an' slow out onto the porch."

He took Eddie out, stuffed the Remington back into his pants, and picked up both the shotgun and the bag.

"All right, back inside."

Eddie complied, albeit reluctantly.

Once in, Longarm broke open the action of the shotgun, opened the box of shells—they were number five, squirrel loads, not that it mattered—and dropped two shells in. He took another handful and put them in his coat pocket. The bulge was not stylish, but style was not what he was after.

"Back outside now, kid."

Eddie did not protest this time, but it was obvious he was not happy with his captor.

Longarm took his prisoner out onto the porch, eared back the hammers of the twelve-gauge, pointed the gun toward the sky, and tripped first one trigger and then the other.

Both barrels fired properly. But then he'd had to try them to make sure. He took the gun and Eddie back inside, shucked the empties out of the gun, and reloaded both barrels.

"Sit down, Eddie."

"Why?"

"'Cause I damn well told you to, that's why."

Eddie sat. Stiffly, but he sat.

Longarm took the roll of light wire from the bag and started wrapping. The gun. Eddie Curen's neck. Around and around until the shotgun muzzle was pressed hard beneath Eddie's throat, the gun held in place there by yards and yards of wire that affixed the gun in place.

"Damn you, you son of a bitch!" Eddie whined.

Longarm's knuckles speared him hard in the kidney. "Oh. Sorry," Longarm said, deadpan. "That was an accident."

"Bullshit," Eddie snapped.

"You want another?"

"My father . . ."

"Is gonna go behind bars, just like you are," Longarm finished for him.

With the shotgun virtually hanging from Eddie Curen's throat, Longarm took his prisoner back to the front door. "Good," he said. "It looks like your chariot awaits, princess."

"Watch how you talk to me, you bastard."

Longarm had another wee accident with his knuckles. "Sorry. They just seem to get away from me sometimes."

"You aren't going to get away with this, you know."

"If I don't, you'll never know about it, because an ounce of squirrel shot will take the top of your head off an' you'll be dead before your knees buckle. Now, shut up and let's go out to that buggy."

Chapter 53

With Eddie reluctantly in tow, Longarm checked first the mule and then the buggy. A horseshoe nail could have been driven into the quick of one of the mule's feet to lame the animal. An axle nut could have been loosened on the buggy to cause a wheel to fall off. There were any number of ways the rig could have been sabotaged, but everything appeared to be all right.

"Get in," he ordered Eddie. "Now slide over to the left. No, you ain't driving, but I want my left hand on those triggers as I'm handier with my right." He grinned. "In case I have to shoot somebody other'n you."

It was awkward for the two of them to crawl onto the buggy seat while Longarm maintained his hold on the shotgun, but they managed to do it with a little wiggling.

Longarm looked around. He saw no one, but he was sure they were being watched. That was fine. Let Ed Senior and his people watch all they liked, just so they kept their distance.

He did not think they would start shooting. Not with Eddie's life in the balance.

But Ed would do *some*thing. Longarm was equally sure of that. After all, the man's whole future, perhaps his own life, depended on it.

"All right, kid. Let's go to Denver."

Longarm picked up the driving lines. It was not easy getting them sorted and in a comfortable position with only one hand to work with, but he was in no hurry now.

He could not easily get to his pocket watch. His hands were rather completely occupied between Eddie on his left and the lines in his right hand, but a glance toward the sky suggested it was early afternoon, call it one o'clock or thereabouts.

That should put him into Fairplay after dark sometime.

"Hyah, mule. Hyup." He shook the lines, and the mule obediently stepped out into an easy walk.

"Wait. Stop."

He drew back on the lines to stop the mule.

Rebecca was running down the middle of the street, waving at them and calling for Longarm to stop.

"What is it, lass?" he asked when she came close.

"You have to take me with you," she said, breathless from the running.

Longarm lifted an eyebrow.

"Ed knows I was your Judas goat, Marshal. He knows I brought Eddie to you so you could capture him. If I stay here, he will kill me. Probably kill me himself." She shuddered. "You have to take me with you. Please. Please, God, or I'll surely die."

"I hadn't thought about that," Longarm admitted. He looked at Eddie and then at the buggy seat. The rig was built for two. But it could hold three in a pinch.

"Tell you what. Crawl up on the luggage shelf in back. You can ride there and keep an eye on our back trail. If you see anyone following us, let me know." He shrugged. "You won't be comfortable, but I can't put him back there. I have to keep hold of this shotgun. Is that all right?"

"I may not be comfortable, but I'll be alive," Rebecca said. "Hold on while I get a comb and a few things." She dashed off and into her house. She came back mere moments later and climbed onto the package shelf behind the buggy's canvas-and-isinglass back.

"Are you set?" he called to her.

"Yes. Let's go."

Once again he shook the lines and set the patient mule into motion.

Chapter 54

"Marshal?"

"What d'you want, Rebecca?"

"There is someone following us. He is, oh, about a half mile back. I keep getting glimpses of him though he never really shows himself."

"That's all right. At the very least Curen will want to keep track of us," Longarm answered.

"My father—" Eddie began, but Longarm cut him off short with a shake of the shotgun.

"Jesus!" Eddie blurted. "Don't *do* that. I thought you were going to pull the trigger."

"Now, that would be a convenience, it's true," Longarm told him, "but it'd be apt to blow slimy brains all over me, and I ain't got no clean clothes without my carpetbag." He sighed. "No idea where it might've got to. Probably I won't never see it again."

"I hope my father's men kill you," Eddie snarled.

"You ain't the first to want someone to do that," Longarm said. "So far nobody's been able to do the job though. Now, shut up. We're coming to the main road down to Manitou."

"Are we really going to Manitou?" Rebecca asked. "I thought you said we were going to Denver."

"We are going to Denver. By way of Fairplay. I was hoping to confuse Ed Senior's people when I said Manitou. Doesn't make any difference now that you say there's somebody following. He'll see right off which way we turn on the old road."

Longarm kept the mule plodding straight ahead when they reached the road that would have taken them down toward Florissant and the Ute Pass road to Manitou and Colorado Springs and the railroad north.

"How's our friend doing back there?" he asked.

"He's . . . he's coming closer. Oh, no, Marshal. He has a bunch of other men with him. They're running their horses. And they have guns. I can see them waving rifles in the air. Oh, Lord, Marshal, I'm scared."

There was no good place out here for him to fort up. Longarm did the best he could by pulling the buggy off the open road and into a stand of pine.

"Out," he said, dragging Eddie out with him. "Rebecca, I want you to get down on the ground underneath the buggy. It ain't much protection, but 'not much' is better'n no protection.

"You," he said, jerking Eddie's shotgun tether, "you an' me are gonna have to settle this here, I reckon." His grin was wicked. "If you're a prayin' man, now would be a good time, because if your daddy's boys are all that set on keepin' him out of jail, you may have to die for them to do it."

"Oh, God," Eddie blurted.

"Exactly," Longarm said.

"What?"

"Never mind. Just come with me beside that dead pine tree. It looks like a good spot to shield us from one side anyhow. Now come on. They'll be on us in no more'n a few seconds."

Chapter 55

The riders, a dozen or more of them, quickly caught up and swept around until they surrounded Longarm on all sides.

He stood about five yards from the halted buggy, where Rebecca was hiding beneath the vehicle. Eddie Curen was still wired firmly to the shotgun. Longarm kept his hold on the twelve-gauge with his left hand.

Longarm watched, seemingly unconcerned, while the Curen Town posse took up their positions around him.

The riders made no move to close in or to overpower him, and none of the men bothered to speak or to threaten with their weapons. They simply sat their horses and waited.

A minute or so later Longarm discovered what they were waiting for. Ed Curen, Sr., himself and in the flesh, rode up in a phaeton pulled by a pair of matched blacks.

Curen's driver pulled the big vehicle inside the ring of riders and stopped half a dozen yards from Longarm's buggy.

"I can't let you go down there and ruin my career," Curen said when he stepped out of the phaeton. "I just can't."

"You're willing to let your son die for that?" Longarm asked.

"Papa, don't let him hurt me. Papa? Please, Papa, don't

let him." Longarm could feel Eddie's trembling through the hold he had on the butt of the shotgun.

"You won't shoot him," Ed said.

"Even if I don't want to," Longarm returned, "my dead finger would drag the triggers down if I was to fall. The result would be the same, wouldn't it? Eddie wouldn't have no head left. It'd all be jelly."

"I can't believe you would do that," the father said again.

Longarm merely shrugged. "So what is it you have in mind here, Ed? You didn't come out here for nothin'. You want me to stop here. How is it you figure to do that, Ed?"

"I want . . . I want to do this without violence if possible. I would be willing to pay you well to simply let Eddie go. No one outside of this little group need ever know, and none of them would ever talk. I can guarantee you that. You can just report that he slipped away from you."

"That would leave you open to blackmail," Longarm said. "You know that, don't you?"

"That would be my problem, not yours. How much would it take, Long? I've offered five thousand for your head. I would double that if you would just let Eddie go. Ten thousand dollars, Long. Think about that. A man could live high on the hog for years with ten thousand dollars."

Longarm shook his head. "No sale, Ed."

"Twenty . . . twenty-five thousand then. Twenty-five thousand dollars in cash. You would be a rich man, Long."

"Make him do it, Papa." Eddie sounded to Longarm like he was just about to the edge, like he might pass out at any moment.

If he did that, Longarm feared, he would drag Longarm's arm down with him and touch off those shotgun barrels whether Longarm wanted it or not.

And if that happened, it was sure to result in a bloodbath. With most of the blood being supplied by Longarm himself.

"Steady, kid," Longarm whispered. "Lean up against that

tree. Don't fall down or we're all done for." He nudged Eddie with his hip, moving the young man over to the dead pine.

"Think about it, Long. Take the money. No one need ever know," Ed urged.

"I'd know" was Longarm's simple answer. "I wouldn't never be able to look in a mirror again."

"You would be rich," Ed said soothingly.

"There's things more important than money, Ed."

"Make him do it, Papa."

"I think I have a solution," Ed said.

"So do I," Longarm responded. "Just you an' your boys turn around an' go home. I'll take Eddie down to Denver and the law will take its course. No one will get hurt."

"You won't charge me with anything?" Ed asked.

"We'll talk about that after I get Eddie safe behind bars with no shotgun tied under his chin," Longarm said.

Ed sighed and shook his head. "You would ruin me, Long. I have . . . I have plans. Wonderful plans. But I need to have a political base for them to happen. U.S. marshal first. Then district attorney. Attorney general of the state. Then on to Washington and higher office. Important office. You mustn't ruin that for me, Long. You mustn't."

"And Eddie?"

"I don't . . . I can't let you ruin everything, Long."

"Papa! Please."

"Let him go, Long. I'll pay you whatever you like. Anything."

"Not gonna happen, Ed."

Curen turned and walked back to the phaeton. He stood there with his back to Longarm, head down and shoulders slumped.

"*Papa!*"

After a full minute or perhaps even longer, Ed turned back around.

He had a revolver in his hand.

Chapter 56

"No, I am not going to shoot you now and let you kill my son," Curen said. "But I can't let you destroy me either, so I have a suggestion."

"I'm listenin'," Longarm said, wary of what the man might have in mind.

"I say we should settle this like gentlemen," Curen said. "I think . . . I think we should have a duel."

Longarm looked around at the ring of Curen's posse who surrounded them.

"No, I . . . would send them away," Curen said. "It would be just the two of us. Not one of those stupid quick-draw confrontations. That would be unfair. I couldn't possibly hope to compete with you about that. No, what I have in mind is an old-fashioned duel. Face-to-face, ten yards apart. One shot per man."

Longarm looked around the ring of riders. "What about them?" he asked.

"I would send them away. You would release Eddie from that . . . thing you have wired under his chin. Just the two of us, Long, and let the best man win."

"Face-to-face, man-to-man?" Longarm asked.

Curen nodded. "Exactly."

Longarm looked up toward the sky to the west. It would be dark soon.

"Send your boys away," he told Ed Senior. "You go with 'em. Give me a half hour, then you come back by yourself. You and me can settle this thing then if you like."

Curen raised his voice. "You heard him, men. Go home. I won't need you any longer, and don't worry. You will all get your pay for today's work."

The riders complied without a quarrel. But then they had no dog in this hunt. They were only in it for the pay.

Curen climbed into the phaeton. He stood there for a moment watching his men head back toward Curen Town; then he said to Longarm, "You will be here when I get back?"

"You have my word on it," Longarm said.

Curen nodded. He sat and called to his driver, "Take me back to town, Jerry."

Rebecca crawled out from beneath the buggy and asked, "Are they really going?"

"Sure looks like it. If they got something up their sleeves, we'll find out about it in due time," Longarm told her.

"What about me?" Eddie wanted to know.

"I'm gonna wire you to that tree," Longarm said. "Understand, though. If your pa has something funny in mind, I'll kill you sure. Even if he has somebody put lead in me, I will make it my last move to kill you."

Eddie shuddered and began to blubber. Longarm ignored that and started removing the yards of wire that secured the shotgun beneath Eddie's chin, using the same wire to tie Eddie against the dead pine.

He handed the shotgun to Rebecca and said, "If Ed doesn't play this straight, girl, I want you to shoot Ed or Eddie or, hell, the both of 'em. But make sure you get at least one, preferably Ed, because he's the one would have you killed if he lives an' I don't."

"You can count on me," Rebecca said.

"Becca. Sweetheart. You know I was going to marry you. I still would," Eddie said.

Rebecca ignored him. But then Eddie and his father and for that matter Curen Town were all yesterday so far as Rebecca Thorn was concerned. She was a girl who knew how to look out for herself, and the Curens were no part of that now.

She stepped over to Eddie, tied securely to the dead pine, and pressed the muzzles of the shotgun into his belly.

"I'm ready," she told Longarm.

"Good, 'cause here comes Ed."

Chapter 57

It was obvious that Ed was not accustomed to driving a two-up team. He handled the lines awkwardly, sending the horses into each other and then away, letting them wander from side to side and—once in a while—down the proper tracks.

"Helluva job," Longarm muttered under his breath.

He watched the phaeton draw close and then swing around so it was facing away from him and the buggy.

He smiled a little.

Ed Curen was driving himself this time. He looked carefully around, then stepped down from the driver's box.

"All right, Long. Are you ready?"

"I reckon so, Ed. You?"

Curen nodded. "I have my pistol here. You are welcome to inspect it if you wish."

For a moment Longarm thought Curen might have the next round chambered with bird or snake shot, intending for it to get into his eyes and blind him. Then the boss of Curen Town came over to stand close to Longarm for a moment, trying to stare him down.

Which Longarm thought was rather funny in as much as Ed Curen was a good head shorter than Longarm and had to crane his neck and practically come up onto tiptoes to look at Longarm's eyes.

Longarm managed to contain his laughter. Hell, that would have been insulting, and he had no desire to do that. "Anytime," he said.

"Very well," Curen said. "You stand, um, here, I think. And I will pace off ten paces. When I am ready, I will call the proper instructions. That is: Cock. Present. Fire."

"All right," Longarm said. "That sounds fine to me."

Curen rather ostentatiously flexed his shoulders and began pacing, counting his steps in a loud voice. He had a revolver of some sort in his belt, a Starr perhaps, but he made no move to draw it yet.

". . . eight . . . nine . . . ten." The little man turned and looked toward Longarm, who motioned for him to wait.

"What is it, Long?" Curen shouted.

"There's somethin' I got to do first." Longarm smiled and touched the brim of his Stetson in apology, then walked over to Rebecca. "If you don't mind, lass, I'll swap you that scattergun for the Remington here."

The girl looked puzzled, but she did not question him. She pulled the shotgun muzzles away from Eddie's belly, turned the gun around, and handed it to Longarm, who in turn gave her the Remington .44-40. "All right, thanks."

Longarm walked back to the spot where he had been standing, but instead of facing Ed Curen, he stood facing the back of the phaeton.

"What are you doing?" Curen shouted.

Longarm waved to him and pointed the gaping tubes of the twelve-gauge toward the black leather drape that covered the luggage boot on the handsome phaeton. "Just checking somethin'," Longarm shouted.

"*No!*" Ed Curen bellowed.

The leather cover was swept aside, and two men tried to uncoil themselves from their cramped position—Lord knew how long they had been crouched in there—and to aim their rifles at the same time.

They were just a little bit slow.

Longarm's first charge of squirrel shot took the man on the left full in the face. At that close range it just did not leave much behind, as most of the meat was turned into red mush, with bits of starkly white bone showing through.

The second shot followed immediately behind the first, the load of twelve-gauge number five shot striking the man on the right in the belly and doubling him over. He slid as much as fell out onto the ground, everything other than his own misery forgotten.

Longarm whirled back around to face Curen, but the man was so mesmerized by Longarm's quick gunfire that he seemed for the moment to have forgotten the revolver that dangled from his own fingers.

"Now, Ed," Longarm said pleasantly, "let's the two of us finish this duel thing, shall we?"

"I, oh . . . Jesus, I . . . I . . ."

"You might wanna drop that pistol," Longarm invited, "lest I think you're fixing to use it."

The revolver fell from suddenly nerveless fingers. The muzzle struck the toe of Curen's boot, but he did not appear to have noticed.

Longarm grunted and apologized. "I'm sorry, Ed, but my other handcuffs is in my carpetbag, and Lord knows what you've done with that."

He sidled over to the tree where Eddie was wired in place and began unwinding the yards of wire. It would just have to do until he got his prisoners down to Denver.

Half an hour later, Longarm was on the driving box of the phaeton while Rebecca, armed with a brace of revolvers, sat in the plush rear-facing seat, and both Ed Senior and Eddie Junior were trussed up and sitting on the front-facing seat.

The mule, still in the poles of the doctor buggy, was tied on at the back of the phaeton.

"If either of 'em moves," Longarm said to her, "pull both triggers an' get outa the way, 'cause I'll be spilling more blood than I really want to. Are you ready, lass?"

She nodded. "Whenever you are, Marshal."

"Then let's us head for Fairplay an' on to Denver." He shook the driving lines and clucked the matched pair of driving horses into motion.

GIANT-SIZED ADVENTURE FROM
AVENGING ANGEL LONGARM.

BY TABOR EVANS

2006 Giant Edition:

LONGARM AND THE
OUTLAW EMPRESS

2007 Giant Edition:

LONGARM AND
THE GOLDEN EAGLE
SHOOT-OUT

2008 Giant Edition:

LONGARM AND THE
VALLEY OF SKULLS

2009 Giant Edition:

LONGARM AND THE
LONE STAR TRACKDOWN

2010 Giant Edition:

LONGARM AND THE
RAILROAD WAR

2013 Giant Edition:

LONGARM AND
THE AMBUSH AT HOLY
DEFIANCE

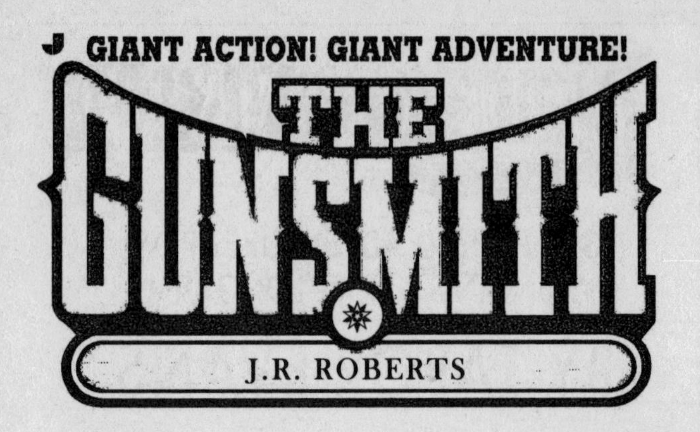

Little Sureshot and the Wild West Show (Gunsmith Giant #9)

Red Mountain (Gunsmith Giant #11)

The Marshal from Paris (Gunsmith Giant #13)

Andersonville Vengeance (Gunsmith Giant #15)

Dead Weight (Gunsmith Giant #10)

The Knights of Misery (Gunsmith Giant #12)

Lincoln's Revenge (Gunsmith Giant #14)

The Further Adventures of James Butler Hickok (Gunsmith Giant #16)